THE PRINCESS OF TIME

TONY CONTRATTO

The Second Book of
The Agents of Fate Series

Hensley de Vere Press
Lake Havasu City, AZ

ISBN 979-8-98860903-2 (Paperback)

Library of Congress Control Number: 2023918530

First paperback edition November 2023

Cover art by: Gennadiy Poznyakov, Bolivia Inteligente
(used under license)

Edited by: Kim Beckham

Printed in the United States of America

Hensley de Vere Press LLC
1799 Kiowa Ave
Suite 111
Lake Havasu City, AZ 86403
hensleydevere.com
contact@hensleydevere.com

Dedication

To the long, winding road that brings the people
we come to know and love into our lives.

Madison

Gracie

Xander

Zaine

Conner

Harrison

CONTENTS

Chapter One 1
 - Alea Iacta Est -
Chapter Two 47
 - Homecoming -
Chapter Three 75
 - The Abassilon Prophecy -
Chapter Four 93
 - Celestial Bodies -
Chapter Five 109
 - Daylight -
Chapter Six 139
 - Moira -
Chapter Seven 187
 - Amira al-Dahr -
Chapter Eight 235
 - End of Days -
Chapter Nine 245
 - The Forbidden Spell -
Chapter Ten 257
 - The Quickening of the Amulet -
Epilogue 273

Appendix I 287
Appendix II 291
Appendix III 295

Preface

Although the general ideas and themes for **The Princess of Time** came to me years ago when I began the concept for **Agents of Fate**, the finer nuances of the story have just recently come into creation.

The first book saw our "hero" Hayden de Vere acquire amazing powers, altering his otherwise normal life forever. He faced tests of strength, fortitude, and ingenuity. Hayden saw several friends and acquaintances fall to the evil machinations of the Alva'ci. Defying the odds, he emerged from the trials victorious. In this new entry to The Agents of Fate Series, we will see Hayden and his group of friends tested once again.

Though they may seem to be, heroes are not infallible. Hayden and the other agents of fate are no exception. As we encounter traumatic and life altering events, we make choices. Among many other plot threads, this book will ask the question of what is right versus wrong. Can we say for certain how we would react given a set of circumstances? How about when those circumstances are coupled with continuous life-or-death decisions?

As always, be on the lookout for easter eggs and small hints of what is to come. If you haven't read the prequel story **The Distant Shadow** yet, make sure to get it for FREE at agentsoffate.com

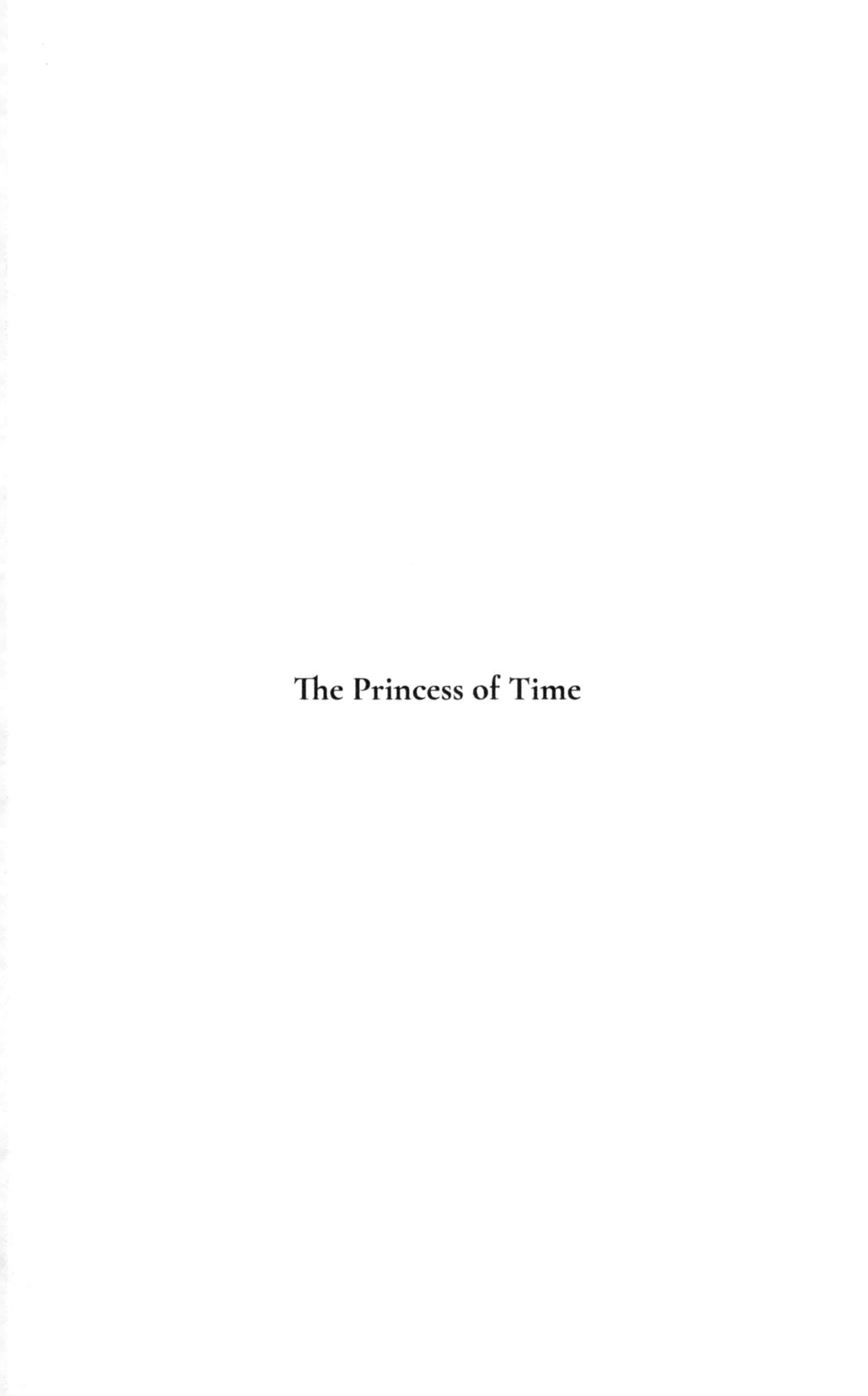

The Princess of Time

أ

Chapter One

Alea Iacta Est

ayden looked at the calendar hanging on the wall in his apartment's kitchen as he poured several glasses of iced tea for his guests. It read January 25, 2023. It had been just over one month since he had finally created a portal large enough and stable enough to transport himself to other locations. Dan and Abby still reminded him almost daily of the grand spectacle he had caused in New York by diving from the top of a skyscraper to test their theory on using increased portal entry speed to achieve jumps of longer distances. Hayden continued to think about the developments he had made in the past month.

After repeated testing, he found that their guesses had been partially correct. However, he was perturbed by the fact that the Alva'ci could cover vast distances through a portal by simply walking through it when it had kidnapped Kali. Hayden concluded that the ability must be somewhat tied to the user's power level. He spent several nights attempting to test his theory by using the dreamscape to focus his connection with the amulet. Though he found that his idea had indeed been correct, he was only able to shave the portal entry speed requirement down by 250 miles per hour. Though it was definite progress, he remained determined to better himself in preparation for an inevitable fight with the Alva'ci to rescue Kali.

Hayden had decided that he would only attempt the jump and resulting battle with the Alva'ci once he was fully confident that he would be successful. To this end, he spent countless hours inside the dreamscape, drawing more and more power from the amulet. He tested himself constantly by creating apparitions of the Alva'ci within the dreamscape and fighting them. Hayden lost the simulated battles after prolonged fighting during the first several attempts. Eventually, he was able to work his way up to a stalemate. He would exit the dreamscape frustrated that neither opponent would come out on top after hours of relentless back and forth.

During a much-needed break from his continuous

preparations, Abby and Dan helped Hayden brainstorm ideas to break through the plateau that was now plaguing his efforts. After a few hours of drinks at Eduardo Quesada's, the three friends had come up with and shot down dozens of ideas. Abby nonchalantly rolled a thought off her tongue that she was half sure would be just another proposal to add to the existential waste basket of ideas.

Hayden paused and thought silently for a few moments to ponder Abby's idea, stopping mid-sip of his beer, before asking her to repeat herself and elaborate.

"Instead of only trying to use the amulet to increase your powers, why don't you try to use your powers to increase the amulet's?" Abby repeated with additional clarification. "If the amulet was more powerful, it would, in turn, increase your power."

Hayden continued to think for a few minutes before he stood from his barstool. He chugged the remainder of his beer and grabbed Abby's hand, leading her outside the bar to the sidewalk with Dan following behind them. Hayden placed the amulet on a park bench in front of them. Dan and Abby stood by, restless in anticipation of what Hayden had planned.

The amulet began to glow faintly as Hayden closed his eyes and pointed his fingers at it. Abby watched in amazement as Hayden etched several words into the amulet with a stream of red-hot fire. After the amulet had cooled, Hayden lifted it from the bench and held it in his palm so that Abby and Dan could see it. Hayden waved his hand over the stone, making the freshly inscribed words glow so they would be easier to read.

Abby read the words aloud. "Emiratus, Youlvasius. Two of the seven spells."

Hayden placed the amulet back around his neck, and the three friends returned to their seats inside the restaurant. They decided to finish their night out before testing the results of Abby's idea. When the trio returned to Hayden's apartment three hours later, he asked them if they wanted to be present as he made another attempt in the dreamscape. Abby and Dan readily agreed to the proposition. However, the group decided to wait until morning when they were all well-rested.

The following day, Hayden woke Abby and Dan. They had both stayed the night at his apartment so they wouldn't have to travel back and forth to their own places. The three friends quickly ate a small breakfast and took turns showering before reassembling in the living room. After settling on the couch, Hayden pulled Abby and Dan into the dreamscape with him.

The surrounding scene inside the dreamscape was a simple construct. A flat expanse of pavement that stretched as far as the eye could see. No foliage or decoration complimented the landscape. Abby and Dan found themselves standing on a raised platform about thirty feet away from Hayden. As they took in the desolate landscape, which differed starkly from the first time their friend had brought them into the dreamscape, Hayden snapped his fingers, and a frighteningly realistic version of the Alva'ci appeared. Hayden looked back at his friends and gave them a thumbs-up gesture. The battle then began without further delay.

At first, Hayden fought at the normal power levels he had managed to achieve over the past few weeks. The battle was still seemingly at the point of stalemate, with neither opponent able to gain a clear upper hand. Hayden drew the amulet from inside his shirt, and the etched spells began to glow fiery red just before the amulet itself started to shine with a bright orange glow. Hayden resumed his attacks on the simulated Alva'ci.

The renewed battle began explosively. Abby and Dan could see from their platform in the distance that the Alva'ci was now at a distinct disadvantage. It had seemed that the idea Abby had posed to the group the previous night was paying off. The amulet's powers and its enhancements from Hayden's modifications appeared to provide a continual loop of increasing strength. Though the apparition of the Alva'ci fought desperately, within minutes, Hayden's newfound depth of power vaporized the being.

After taking a moment to savor the victory, Hayden pulled the trio out of the dreamscape. When they woke in the living room of Hayden's apartment, Abby excitedly pulled Hayden and Dan into a group hug to celebrate the breakthrough.

☙ ☙ ☙ ☙ ☙ ☙

Hayden snapped back into the moment. He carried the glasses of iced tea into the living room and distributed them to Abby, Dan, and Armond before making a return trip to retrieve his own beverage. As he squeezed a slice of lemon into his tea, Hayden began summarizing his plans for the following day.

"So tomorrow, we all only have one class in the morning," Hayden said before sipping his tea. "We can all meet here afterward and go over any last-minute strategy. Then, I will open a portal to the planet where the Alva'ci is holding Kali. I don't know how long I will be gone. I don't expect any of you to wait around, but you are all welcome to stay here as long as it takes."

"I'll probably just stay here," Abby told Hayden. "I want to be here as soon as you bring Kali back."

"Well, I have to win first," Hayden reminded her.

"I have no doubt that you'll win," she replied confidently. "Dan and I saw what you did in the dreamscape a week ago. You won then, and you've spent the last several days working on drawing even more power from the amulet."

☙ ☙ ☙ ☙ ☙ ☙

The next morning's class passed quickly. Hayden found that he was concentrating more on his looming mission to save Kali than on what the professor was teaching. He met the group back at his apartment to prepare for his impending departure into the unknown.

"Remember, you must be prepared for anything to happen," Armond cautioned Hayden. "We do not know how much the Alva'ci has recovered since it has been gone. It may be even more powerful than before since it has access to one of its old home planets."

"I know. I am expecting the worst but hoping for the best," Hayden replied.

"You've become a lot more powerful, too," Abby reminded him. "We all have confidence in you. We know that you'll succeed and bring Kali home."

"I just hope that I'm not too late after spending all of this time preparing," Hayden said, trying to hide the emotion behind the grim possibility.

As the group ate lunch, a quiet and somber mood lingered in the apartment. After finishing, Hayden rose from his chair and led Dan, Abby, and Armond outside to the front yard.

"Well, this is it," Hayden told his group of friends. "It is time to get this done."

"Good luck," Abby responded, with Dan and Armond nodding their heads in agreement. "We will be here when you get back."

Each of his friends exchanged a quick hug with Hayden before he readied himself to leave. They watched as Hayden's feet left the ground, and he slowly rose into the air above his apartment. After a final farewell wave, Hayden ascended more quickly and flew off into the distance. Dan, Abby, and Armond kept their eyes on the sky in anticipation of the coming spectacle. A few seconds later, the sound and force of the shockwave rattled nearby windows as Hayden broke the sound barrier on his return approach. When

Hayden reappeared above them, he was flying through the air with immense speed. A portal opened in front of him and Hayden vanished into the field.

"I guess now we wait," Dan told the others as they ventured back inside Hayden's apartment. "Can't believe that Clark and Samantha missed this."

"I'm sure they would have loved to see that," Abby replied. "But Clark couldn't pass up that job offer in Illinois."

☜ ☜ ☜ ☜ ☜ ☜

Later that night, Hayden's apartment was quiet. Though Dan was fast asleep on the pull-out bed in the living room, and Armond was presumably the same in the guest bedroom, Abby was finding that she was too restless to doze off. As she lay in the darkness, staring at the ceiling above Hayden's bed, she found her mind inexplicably wandering to memories of the last time she had been in that bed.

Abby had met Hayden and Dan during her very first week at the university. She was in the campus bookstore attempting to find textbooks for her inaugural freshman semester. Hayden had approached her, noticing that she looked lost in the sea of bookshelves.

"Need any help?" he asked her, Dan walking up

shortly after to join them. "We've done this song and dance a few times now."

"Are you sure?" Abby questioned, not wanting to burden her new acquaintances with her problems.

"Yeah, of course," Hayden reassured her, holding out his hand to request that she give him her list of required books. "We've got plenty of time, and I remember being in your shoes during my first week."

"Is it that obvious I'm new here?" Abby asked sheepishly, now dreading the fact that she was apparently giving off newcomer vibes.

"Yeah," Dan replied. "It's all good, though. I'm pretty sure I looked like a lost toddler in a mall the first time I stepped foot in here."

Hayden analyzed the list of books for a moment. "I'm Hayden, by the way, and this is Dan."

"It's really good to meet you guys," she responded, feeling distinctly lucky to find two helpful and friendly people amidst the crowd of others filling the store. "My name is Abby Foster."

"Where are you from, Abby?" Hayden asked her as he started walking through the crowds of people toward another section of the bookstore.

"I'm from Saint George, Utah."

"Interesting," Hayden replied. "What brings you to Fullerton for school?"

"I went to a lecture back in my town by one of the computer science professors here, and it was fascinating," Abby excitedly told her story. "So I flew out here for a campus tour last year and ended up really liking the place. Plus, my aunt lives in Brea, so she's letting me stay with her until I can get a job and afford my own place."

"Alright, that's a much better story than I've heard from other people," Hayden told her as he pulled a series of books from a shelf and handed them to her. "That should do it. The last book on the list, our friend Paige still has a copy. She'll let you borrow it for the semester."

"Really?" Abby said, surprised and questioning why someone she hadn't met would loan her a book that cost $189.

"Yeah, don't worry about it," Hayden once again reassured her as he led the way to the registers to check out. "Save that money and get something more exciting than a textbook."

"Thank you both for helping me!" Abby exclaimed. "You won't even believe how scared I was that I would go all semester without making any friends."

After paying for her textbooks, Abby apologized to Hayden and Dan for needing to abruptly depart in order to make it to her next class on time. Before she left, she gave Hayden her phone number.

"I'll text you when I get that book from Paige, and we can meet up somewhere so I can give it to you," he informed her.

"Okay, thank you, Hayden," Abby replied. "Maybe this evening we can all go have dinner together and hang out if you guys aren't busy?"

"Sure," Hayden responded. "I'll text you after Dan and I get out of our physics class."

Abby waved as she walked away across the quad. She was delighted that she had seemingly avoided the realization of her fear of feeling alone by attending college in a town far away from home. Her next class was shorter than usual since the professor only concentrated on reviewing the syllabus and doing brief introductions. Abby soon found herself alone in the student union eating lunch. She was observing the crowds of other students, all buzzing about with their groups of friends, when her phone chimed in her pocket.

Hayden had texted and invited her to join his group of friends at a nearby restaurant that she would soon learn was a mainstay in their culinary traditions. She texted him back that she would definitely attend the outing. As the afternoon rolled on, Abby began preparing at her aunt's house. After a quick shower, she deliberated on an outfit, casting aside several potentials before ultimately deciding on a casual yet cute baby blue dress.

Abby arrived at the restaurant to find Dan and Hayden in the parking lot. They were standing near the entrance to the building with three other people. As Abby walked up and approached the group, she waved to Hayden, hoping he would see her and alert the others that she was not a random stranger. Upon seeing her, Hayden immediately walked over to Abby and brought her into the group.

"Guys, this is Abby," Hayden relayed to the three unfamiliar faces, then continued the introductions. "Abby, this is Clark, Samantha, and Paige. Obviously, you already know Dan from earlier today. Oh, and I didn't forget about that book. Paige has it in her car for you."

"Thank you, Paige," Abby immediately said. "It's so nice of you to let me borrow your textbook. You don't even know how much I appreciate it."

"You're welcome," Paige replied. "I'm happy it will be getting much better use than just sitting on my shelf at home."

Hayden led the group inside, and they enjoyed a couple hours of hanging out and discussing the particulars of their first week of the semester so far. When Abby arrived back at her aunt's house later in the evening, she was content that her outlook for college life was trending positive.

The next day after her midday English class, Abby spent fifteen minutes deliberating on the wording of a text message before finally hitting the send button. For all of the time spent erasing and re-typing the message, she had simply asked Hayden what he was doing that evening. He replied that he had no plans other than, perhaps, doing some homework. Abby shot another message back asking if he wanted to go out and grab dinner.

"Everyone or just us?" Hayden texted back to her.

Abby hesitated for a few moments before she replied. "Just us...?" Now, she was nervous. It seemed like forever to her before Hayden replied.

"Yeah, I'd be happy to. Any preference on what to eat?"

"Just something casual," Abby sent. "Somewhere you think is good."

"Alright, for casual, we can do Flame Broiler. You want to meet there… or want me to pick you up?"

"If it's not an inconvenience to you," Abby typed. "I'll ride with you."

"It's not a problem at all," Hayden replied. "I'll pick you up at 7:00 p.m. Just text me your address."

Abby smiled as she sent the address for her aunt's

house over to him. She walked to her car with a little more excitement in her step as she left campus to begin getting ready. Hayden arrived at her aunt's house right on time, and Abby came outside to meet him as soon as she saw him pull up.

Even with their meal being interrupted by frequent conversation, dinner was over relatively quickly. Abby expressed her desire to continue hanging out for at least a few more hours. After a trip to get some ice cream for dessert, the two eventually ended up at Hayden's apartment so he could drop off the extra half-gallon of cookies and cream he had bought.

"I'll run this into the freezer and then come back out and take you home," Hayden told her.

"I can come in for a little while," Abby suggested. "I mean, if you still want to hang out with me for longer."

"Yeah, if you want to," Hayden acquiesced. "I'm having a good time. I just don't want you to get the impression that I came here for any reason other than dropping off my ice cream."

Abby gave him a look. "I don't think that," she replied.

Hayden led Abby inside his apartment and asked her to ignore any errant messes, citing first-week-of-classes madness as his reasoning. After a short tour, Abby shared more about her hometown with Hayden. He continued the conversation, telling her more about his background.

"I grew up in Moorpark, about two hours from here. Once I moved down here for college, my parents decided to go stay full-time at their other house in Nevada. I met Dan during freshman year, Clark and Samantha came along last year, and I've been friends with Paige since the end of elementary school."

They continued exchanging stories about their pasts and their college ambitions for the next two hours. The television droned on in the background, though they never actually watched it. Soon they realized that the night was quickly creeping up on 11:00 p.m.

"I totally didn't notice how late it was," Hayden remarked when he glanced at the clock. "I'll get you back over to your aunt's house so you're not dead tired in your classes tomorrow."

As Hayden readied himself to stand up and take her home, Abby decided to follow through with what she had been contemplating for the past hour. She placed her hand on Hayden's chest and stopped him from getting up. The confusion on Hayden's face was quickly dispersed when Abby proceeded to kiss him.

Hayden sat on the couch, surprised, as the kiss ended.

It was apparent to Abby that he thought the kiss was meant as a final capstone to the night. She signaled her intention to stay for at least a little while longer by climbing on top of him and pulling her shirt off. Hayden quickly understood her intentions, and the two found themselves shedding their remaining clothes hurriedly, flinging pieces across the room with no regard for their resting place. Hayden took a moment to make sure that she was comfortable with proceeding any further, to which she enthusiastically agreed.

After having one of the best nights of sleep that Abby could remember in some time, she awoke the next morning to the sound of Hayden's shower running in the adjoining bathroom. She stood up and momentarily wondered where all her clothes were, before remembering that they were strewn all over the front room. Abby approached the bathroom door to find that Hayden was standing in front of the mirror, still nude, and brushing his teeth. She leaned up against the door frame and stared at his body. Hayden immediately noticed her in his peripheral vision and took the moment to return the observational gesture.

"So, do you think I can just ride with you over to the college?" she asked him innocently.

"Of course you can," Hayden insisted, wondering why she even felt the need to ask. "I can also take you to your aunt's house before if we have time."

"I don't think we're going to have time for that. My aunt will almost certainly ask me questions. I don't want to make you late," Abby told him. "But if you don't mind taking me there after class, I would appreciate that."

"Definitely, Abby," he again reassured her, hoping to help Abby move past the point of feeling like she was being a burden by asking for things that should be considered basic decency.

As Hayden opened the shower door and stepped inside, he motioned for Abby to join him. She paused for a moment to consider before realizing how ridiculous she sounded to herself. There was no reason to be bashful or coy after the previous night. She stepped into the steaming hot environment, and Hayden ceded first water rights to her. Abby began to lather her hair with shampoo as Hayden waited for his turn in the water, using the time to watch her intently.

After Abby relinquished her place under the showerhead, the two took turns washing and rinsing. As she stood in front of the mirror to begin getting ready for the day, Hayden went out to the living room and retrieved her clothes.

During her classes that day, Abby lost herself in thought to one of the traits that she despised most about herself: her insecurity. She possessed a nagging uncertainty that she was nothing more than mildly adequate, if that. It was something that she desperately wanted to conquer during her college years, but here she found herself in the very first week, already slipping back into doubting her worth. The inner monologue in her head battled back and forth with itself, trying to convince her to take a step in the direction of believing in herself… even if it meant facing the fear of rejection. The opposing voice reasoned that rejection was the very thing that would send her deeper down the rabbit hole. It reminded her of how alone she had felt during her junior high years and continued in its attempts to gaslight her into remaining the same. As class ended and the other students began filing out of the room, Abby decided that listening to that fear for long enough that she missed an entire lecture was enough to draw the line… at least for the next ten minutes while her courage was galvanized.

"Besides," she thought to herself. "What is it that I'm so afraid of this morning? That Hayden absolutely hated last night and was only acting nice this morning until he could take me to campus and then disappear to never be seen again?"

"Yeah, that's exactly what I'm afraid of," Abby found that intrusive voice slowly creeping in again to derail her motivation. "I'm afraid that although he seems like the nicest person I've met in a long time, that he sees right through me, and it's only a matter of time before my texts are answered by nothing more than a resounding silence. I'm afraid that he only let me stay the night because I was practically begging him."

Abby was frustrated with herself. She was teetering between the intrusive thoughts and the person that she wanted to become. Abby finally decided to send a text while she still had the nerve to do so. However, her indecisiveness was as plain as day when she read the message back to herself after sending it.

"I completely understand if you don't want to… but maybe after you take me to my aunt's, I can come over again?" the text message read.

As she continued to read the message over and over, the intrusive thoughts came back full force in a relentless bout of humiliation. They chipped away at her confidence, trying to destroy the little sense of self-worth she had managed to build in the past few years. They wanted her to avoid being foolish enough to put her feelings on the line again. She was slumped into a chair in the now-vacant hallway of the Humanities Building, so deeply lost in thought that she hardly noticed her cell phone chiming from her lap. The reminder notification went off for the second time and managed to snap her back to reality long enough to see that Hayden hadn't ghosted her… he was texting back. Her hands trembled with fear as she unlocked her phone and looked down at the messaging app.

"Absolutely."

Her mind immediately went back to war with itself.

"See, he really does like me."

"He's just saying that to be nice. Just because he's trying to let you down easy doesn't mean he likes you."

"If he didn't, he wouldn't have texted back."

"He can probably tell that you have issues. Just like I said before, he pities you. He's just looking for an easy moment to escape."

"No, you're wrong. When I was there last night, I could feel that he was being genuine. He enjoyed himself. He enjoyed being with me."

"Listen to yourself. You're so deluded with hope that it's pathetic. You literally threw yourself at him when he was trying to get you to leave. Every guy that's ever tried to date you left before you even got the chance to desperately convince them to stay. This is no different, other than the fact that he saw a chance to get some before he dipped out."

"That's not true."

"Wow, how embarrassing are you? I'll just wait

until you're muffling your cries in your pillow tonight at your aunt's house to say I told you so."

Abby remained on the chair in the hallway… motionless, numb. How long had she been sitting there, she wondered. A tear ran down her cheek.

"Abby!" Hayden said in a raised voice as he gently touched her shoulder. He had tried to get her attention twice before as he was walking down the hallway.

She looked up in shock to see Hayden standing right in front of her. Abby was mortified. She was convinced that this would most certainly be the last straw that sent Hayden running for the hills.

"Are you alright?" Hayden asked her, with concern marking his words. "You hadn't texted me back in like thirty minutes and we were going to swing by your aunt's house after you finished this class… so I decided to come see if it ran late or something."

"Ummm, yeah, I'm fine. I just hit my shin really hard on a cabinet on the way out of the classroom and had to sit down. I guess I lost track of time," she told Hayden, her thoughts convincing her that she had better make something up quick so he wouldn't know the truth.

Hayden looked at her, and she felt like he was peering into her soul, past all the lies. She was becoming more and more sure that he would walk away any second now. Hayden reached out his hand and wiped the tear from her cheek.

"Do you need help walking?" he asked her as he offered his hand to help her up from the chair.

"No, I think I'm alright now," she told him as she slowly stood, wondering why he was still there.

As they exited the building and made their way across campus to the parking lot, Hayden looked over at her and paused in his stride. "You can talk to me, Abby. I just want you to know that."

"Shit, he knows," her thoughts cried out in her head. "Play it cool."

"I know," she eventually replied aloud. "It was just a really rough class today. It has me frustrated."

"Okay," Hayden almost seemed to relent as they started to continue their walk toward his car. "If your English class is giving you trouble, I've been known to write twenty-page term papers hours before they're due and still get an 'A.' I can definitely help you with that. Also, I'm an excellent listener."

That last sentence stung like a blade coated in salt as the words echoed in Abby's ears. He knew something was wrong, but he wasn't going to pressure her to say what it was. The ball was in her court now. She was one hundred percent sure that after tonight, she wasn't just going to lose Hayden in her life; she was also going to lose that entire friend group she had just met. Abby was so despondent that she didn't even bother to respond to Hayden. She simply climbed into the passenger seat of his car and stared out the window. Once again she felt numb, as Hayden drove toward her aunt's house, undoubtedly to say goodbye forever.

Hayden pulled into the driveway of Abby's aunt's home in Brea. For the first time during the silent car ride, she looked over at him. She didn't even try to hide her self-loathing anymore at this point.

"Thanks, Hayden," she somberly said as she prepared to open the car door. "Goodbye."

Hayden sighed as he stared into her eyes. "Abby, I thought you wanted to come over and hang out again tonight. Pardon my asking, but did I do something wrong?"

Just as immediate as a backdraft envelops a room with fire, the voices driving Abby's internal monologue lit ablaze after hearing Hayden's remark.

"He knows it's not him that's fucked up," her intrusive thoughts barked, taking the lead on the conversation in her head. "He knows you're damaged goods, but apparently, he thinks you're good for one thing."

"For once, I kind of agree," the voice that Abby had

dubbed as her voice of reason chimed in. "He didn't do anything wrong, and he knows it. Why is he trying to get you to come back again?"

Finally, Abby vocalized her thoughts to Hayden. "You didn't do anything. You know you didn't do anything wrong. It's me… and you don't need to put yourself through this."

Hayden tried to hide the concern in his words as best he could. He determined that he wasn't going to be able to shift the focus to himself to get Abby to open up. He felt terrible for even attempting it, but he was worried about her. He decided, as a final effort, to just be direct and stern with her.

"Abby, go inside, get a change of clothes, whatever books you need for tomorrow, and anything else you need… and then come back out here and get in the car," Hayden directed her, his voice crisp and certain. "I want to spend time with you. Tonight. I'm going to wait for you right here."

Abby was speechless, as were the proverbial angel and demon on her shoulders. She opened the car door and got out, slowly walking up to the entrance of the house with her head spinning in confusion. She silently wandered down the hallway to her bedroom and sat on the edge of her bed. Luckily, her aunt wasn't home to perform an inquisition. Five minutes passed, and she still hadn't moved. Finally, a thought came to her… "Get the fuck up and do what he said."

Leaping up from her place on the bed, Abby ran to the window and looked through the blinds, fully expecting to see the taillights of Hayden's car disappearing down the road. She couldn't believe that he was still sitting there in the driveway. A rush of adrenaline surged through her body for some reason unknown to her. She grabbed her backpack and shoved her textbooks inside. After thinking for a moment, she walked over to her dresser and pulled the top drawer out like she was attempting to dislodge Excalibur from the stone in Camelot. She quickly grabbed a handful of panties and several bras and added them to her backpack, not even pausing to contemplate why she was bringing so many. A couple of shirts and pairs of pants followed. Her bag now looked like she was packing for a week-long camping trip. Abby stumbled out of her room and into the hallway, stopping in the bathroom to grab her toothbrush and some extra makeup remover wipes.

She walked quickly down the driveway. Her pace noticeably more rapid than when she had walked up it just ten minutes ago to retreat into the house. Abby tried her best to appear calm as she opened the door and sat back down in the passenger seat, though she knew that both her demeanor and her bulging backpack were giving away the fact she was anything but calm.

"I'm sorry if you were about to leave," she said as she sat down, waiting to put her seatbelt on until she was sure Hayden wasn't going to tell her to nevermind after all.

"I wasn't going anywhere, Abby," he replied.

She reached up and grabbed her seatbelt, still not entirely sure but buckling it anyway. Hayden smiled at her and reversed down the driveway. Once again, she found that she didn't know what to say on the ride back to Fullerton. When they arrived at Hayden's apartment, he grabbed Abby's backpack and carried it for her. She was surprised that she was actually walking back into his home. Hayden sat her backpack down on the floor next to the coffee table and then sat next to her on the couch.

"I'm glad that you're here," he told her as he held her in an extended hug.

As much as she wanted to fight it and keep her guard up, Abby sunk into Hayden's embrace. Her confusion as to why he asked her back over still persisted, but at the moment, it didn't matter to her.

"Talk to me, Abby, please?" Hayden asked a few minutes into the hug. "I want you here. Tonight is for whatever you need... I'm not expecting anything to happen tonight except for us talking."

Abby's tears began to flow freely, running from her cheeks onto Hayden's neck and shoulder as he held his grasp on her. Abby wept for ten uninterrupted minutes before she looked up.

"Oh my God, Hayden. I'm so sorry, I completely soaked your shoulder," she said shakily as she saw the large wet spot on his shirt.

"I know, your tears are running down my chest and back," he told her, unfazed. "But that's okay. I want you to get it out so you can open up and talk to me."

Abby was still thoroughly confused as to why Hayden even had her there in his house again. After running the assumed probabilities through her head, she kissed him and began to climb on top of him. Hayden kissed her back but stopped her before she could go any further.

"That's not why I brought you here," he told Abby as he looked her in the eyes. "Talk to me."

Abby then went against what every fiber of her being was telling her to do in the moment and actually spoke.

"I'm a mess, Hayden," she finally relented and began to let her emotions out to someone for the first time that she could even remember. "There's something wrong with me."

"There's nothing wrong with you, Abby," Hayden insisted as he held her hands in his. "But why do you feel like that?"

It was now or never, she decided.

"I know it sounds stupid, but I literally have no self-confidence whatsoever," she continued to open up, much to her own surprise. "The past couple of years, I thought I was doing better. I was feeling a little better about myself, but then this morning, in the shower, I let myself worry, and the rest of the day went downhill drastically. It was like all the progress that I thought I had made went away in an instant. I had told myself that college was going to be my time to finally get over this and be a better person, but I failed at that in my very first week here. I convinced myself today that you weren't going to text me back, that you would just disappear, and that I would lose not only you but Dan, Paige, Clark, and Samantha also. That giant snowball of doom started from just one little thought in the shower."

"What was the thought?" Hayden asked.

"Honestly, it was just something that ran through my head while I watched you rinsing the shampoo out of your hair. I wondered if you had enjoyed what we did the night before… and then that led to me doubting absolutely everything."

"Abby," Hayden stopped her. "Being one-hundred percent honest with you, I enjoyed last night. It was great. I'm not saying that to make you feel better. I'm saying it because it's the truth."

Abby examined Hayden's face as he spoke. He was definitely telling the truth. She let that sink in as she continued to listen to him talk.

"I'm going to say this once right now, but I will say it over and over again until you can say it and know that it's true in your own mind," Hayden paused before continuing, still staring straight into Abby's eyes. "You are worth it. You are important… to me, to our group of friends, to many more people. What you have to give in this life is irreplaceable."

"Fuck," Abby mumbled before the tears erupted again. This time, Hayden didn't let her seek refuge against his shoulder. He grabbed her sides and kept her sitting straight up, still perched on his lap from her misguided assumption that the moment was meant to turn sexual.

"Something happened to make you feel like this, Abby," Hayden postulated. "What was it? When did this begin?"

"I was a happy little girl, I know that," Abby started her confessional. "I was convinced I would grow up to be a princess. I had some friends. The first time I remember feeling like this was when I was twelve. I mean, I was bullied a little with my red hair, of course. But I knew I was going to get called a ginger by all the stupid kids. Something just changed when I was twelve, and I don't know exactly what it was, but ever since then, I wasn't a happy girl anymore."

"Okay, let's figure this out together," Hayden recommended to her. "Do you trust me?"

"Right now, I trust you more than I've trusted anyone in six years," she candidly revealed to Hayden.

"What I want you to do is close your eyes," Hayden began. "I'm going to hold your hands so you can feel me here. Focus on when you were twelve years old. Think about January 1st, New Year's Day. Think about everything you can remember that happened that day. Think about anything you can recall that someone said to you that sticks out in your mind. Then go on to the next day. Tell me anything that comes into your mind. Tell me if you encounter a day or a period of time where you can't remember anything at all."

"Ummmm, okay," Abby said after she heard Hayden's request.

"I know," he told her. "I'm asking you to bare your soul, to expose yourself in some of the most intimate ways possible. Do you trust me?"

Abby answered his question by closing her eyes and beginning. She floated through the first ten days of January, recalling only happy memories. The remainder of that month contained a handful of bad memories... her parents fighting, an older kid teasing her, and her brother stealing her favorite book and throwing it over the fence into the neighbor's pool. The next hour yielded similar results for the months of February through July.

Hayden stopped her for a moment so that he could grab them both a bottle of water. Abby insisted on taking her place back on Hayden's lap when they continued. Abby picked back up on the first of August and worked her way up to the 21st.

"I'm not really getting anything," she admitted after concentrating on the day for a few minutes.

"How about the next day?" Hayden asked.

"The next day was my birthday," she paused momentarily to remember it. "It wasn't a good birthday. I was sad."

"Do you remember why?" Hayden inquired.

"My birthday felt ruined. I felt really bad about myself. It wasn't from anything that happened that day. It was because of the day before."

Abby opened her eyes and looked at Hayden. She was visibly nervous about the fact that she couldn't remember why her twelfth birthday was so bad.

"Go back to the day before, Abby," Hayden instructed her and then guided her through the day to try and reignite her memories. "Close your eyes. You're asleep in bed. It's the last day of being eleven."

Abby pictured herself in her childhood bed, still asleep as daylight peered through the window.

"You wake up. You open your eyes. What do you see and hear? Tell me as you experience it."

"I'm in my room," she started. "I can smell my mother making breakfast from down the hallway. It smells like she is also making coffee. I get up and go to the bathroom to pee and rinse my face off. I walk down the hallway and see my mother cooking. My brother is already sitting at the table eating some pancakes and fruit. I sit down at the table, and my mom brings me some breakfast."

Abby continued to recount the morning with nothing out of the ordinary.

"Okay, now it's noon," she said as she reached midday in the memory. "My brother went down the street to his friend's house to play. I'm in my bedroom. I hear the front door open and then slam shut. My dad is yelling at my mom. I try to play with my toys instead of listening to what's going on down the hall. I hear something break in the kitchen, like a plate or a cup. I walk over to my bedroom door and see my mom running past me down the hallway, she has her hand over her face. I walk down the hallway to see what broke in the kitchen. My dad is standing at the sink, still yelling at my mom, who is in the other room. I wanted to help my mom, so I start to pick up the broken plate off the floor. My dad turns around and starts walking toward me. I don't think he sees me. My dad trips over me and falls on the kitchen floor."

Abby then stopped speaking for a few moments, her face becoming more distraught.

"Hayden… why?" she finally uttered.

"What happened, Abby?" he urged her to continue.

"My dad is angry at me for tripping him, even though I was just trying to help clean up the broken plate," she paused again before continuing. "He grabs me by the hair and lifts me up off the ground. It hurts. He throws me against the wall separating the kitchen from the living room. I'm crying for my mother because my body hurts all over. He's saying something to me…"

Hayden waited for Abby to continue on her own.

"He's telling me that I am useless, just like my mother. That I'm just an ugly little shit that is good for nothing. He is saying that he would have been able to have a happy life if I had never been born and that he wouldn't care if he never saw me again. He just walked out the front door and slammed it."

Abby opened her eyes, and Hayden could see the depth of hurt that had come from recovering that moment in time from within a locked chamber in her mind. Abby just stared at Hayden in silence, shock still gripping her.

"Hayden, I don't even think that my mom heard what he said to me," she admitted when she finally spoke. "You're the only person that knows this about me. Please don't leave me, don't let me be alone with this."

"I'm not going anywhere, Abby," he assured her. "Now you know the why. We're going to work on the rest together, but not tonight. Now, you need to take some time to process. You can talk to me about whatever comes into your mind. You need to rest also."

An hour later, Abby lay awake next to Hayden in his bed. As they talked, she continued to analyze her thoughts from the night. She felt a surge of hope and optimism for her future and a renewed desire to be whole.

"How do I get back to being a regular person again?" Abby asked Hayden as she cuddled next to him, then fired off a salvo of additional questions. "Will you help me? What exactly are we?"

"Of course, I'll help you get there," Hayden told her. "It's just going to take working through what you experienced and changing your mindset that has developed over the years since then. I'm here for you every step of the way. As for us, we can be whatever you want us to be. What I will predict, though, Abby, is that this relationship, romance-wise, more than likely has an expiration date on it. I'm not saying that because I plan on leaving you. I'll be here with you for as long as you need. I'm saying this because one day, you're going to wake up, and you're going to feel whole again. You're going to feel like you're ready to take on the world and conquer it. When that happens, you're going to realize that the only healthy way for us to go on is as friends. Right now, this relationship is rooted in a trauma bond. That type of bond won't be healthy or productive at some point in the future… it could be a month, it could be a year. I don't know when you're going to decide that it's time to go back to just being friends, but just know that I'm here for you until that day, and I'll continue to be there for you after that day. The dynamic of our relationship may change, but the strength of it won't. So let's enjoy what it is right now, and let's cherish what it becomes later."

"Why are you in college to become a doctor, Hayden?" Abby questioned. "With speeches like that, you should be an actor or a politician or something. As for your prediction about me ending what we have going on now… honestly, I don't really see that day ever coming."

"Well, it's hard to see the end of the tunnel when you're lost in the darkness, but it's there," Hayden said. Those words would end up staying with Abby for the rest of her life.

"I know that this is way too much to ask of you," Abby led in with the promise of something significant. "Would it be okay if I moved in with you? I can put all my stuff in the guest bedroom so no one thinks we're together, and you can even banish me to that room if you get tired of me… but I need to be close to you. I'm probably going to be here all the time anyway, so we'd be saving gas money versus driving to Brea and back all the time."

"Because Brea is hundreds of miles away?" Hayden laughed as he joked. "You can move in here, Abby. We can put enough of your stuff in the other bedroom so Dan and everyone else don't go jumping to conclusions. That way, it's easier when you're ready to go. I know department chairs on campus that need student workers, so I can get you hired with one of them with no problem. Then we spend our days learning and our nights making the most of this while we get you where you need to be."

Abby simply hummed a response that conveyed satisfaction with their newly forged plan. She nestled her face against Hayden's neck and pressed her body up against his as she fell asleep, finally feeling peace in a day replete with anguish.

The four months that followed began with Abby explaining to her aunt that she had already found a group of friends and that she couldn't pass up the opportunity to live so close to campus. On nights that Hayden and Abby weren't hanging out with their group of friends, they concentrated on delving into her past and making progress on her mental health.

Christmas Day arrived before anyone could fathom it. As was tradition, the group of friends spent the day together. Abby was overjoyed to celebrate her first Christmas with these people, who just several months ago were strangers but now represented the closest thing she felt to family.

After Hayden and Abby arrived back at the apartment at the conclusion of the holiday festivities, they met in the bathroom to prepare for bed. Hayden waited in the bedroom while Abby finished brushing her teeth. Abby entered the room nude and approached Hayden. As she kissed him, she paused.

"One last Christmas present," she said, but in a tone that didn't readily reflect a notion of cheer and joy to the world.

"I woke up today," she continued. "And I knew what you meant all those months ago. I feel whole again. I feel complete. You and I made that possible together. I also realized that you were right about this relationship having its foundation rooted in my trauma. As much as I enjoy it, if we don't go back to being just friends and we somehow end in the future on bad terms, it would crush me. I understand now exactly what you already knew. I'll always love that about you. You believed in me when I didn't even believe in myself. You gave me the chance to live again. But even though I woke up knowing this, I want one last time."

Hayden smiled at her revelation. "One last time," he agreed.

ဢ ဢ ဢ ဢ ဢ ဢ

Abby drifted from her memory back to the present. As she lay in that bed again for the first time in almost thirteen months, she simply enjoyed the fact that she and Hayden remained close friends, just as they had promised each other. She was also glad that they had agreed to keep their brief tryst a secret from the rest of the friend group during and after its course.

The night she stayed at Hayden's apartment after they crafted the amulet cemented in her mind that they were both genuinely committed to leaving the past as the past. They had successfully transitioned back to a strictly platonic friendship. With that final reflection, Abby finally drifted off to sleep amidst her strangely familiar surroundings.

A bright orange flash illuminated the darkness of space as the portal appeared. Hayden flew out of the field, and it quickly disappeared behind him. As he slowed down to a stop, Hayden observed the scene in front of him. The planet that he had seen before during his initial visualization of the area was in front of him. In orbit of the planet was a large metallic-looking structure. Hayden had detected the signatures of life coming from within back in December, so he decided to begin searching there.

Propelling himself through the darkness, Hayden took mental note of the absolute silence enveloping the vast empty space around him. As he approached the area, Hayden observed what looked like an entrance along the side of the structure. When he arrived, he was confronted with a sensor of some sort to the right of the airlock door. Hayden put his palm up to the sensor, and the back of his hand began to glow with the symbol طاقة. The airlock doors slid open before him.

"So far, this is way too easy," Hayden thought.

He cautiously made his way into the airlock chamber. Hayden's senses were now on high alert. He was entering the literal den of the enemy with no real idea of what he was looking for. All that he did know was that he was in for a fight.

The exterior airlock doors hissed shut behind him as Hayden peered through the thick glass windows surrounding the enclosure. A small light above the interior airlock doors illuminated blue, and suddenly, Hayden's feet made contact with the floor as gravity returned. Sensing no imminent threat, Hayden let his Chantiatus forcefield flicker away. He placed his hand up to the sensor, near the interior doors, and they opened.

Hayden stepped into the chamber before him. As he heard the sound of the doors closing behind him, Hayden flinched as a red light began to flash from points all around the room.

"Shit, I'm going to guess that's an alarm," he said aloud.

Remaining still, Hayden watched for any sign of adversaries. After a minute, he relaxed the tension in his muscles slightly. No one had come to confront him. The only thing he noticed was that a set of doors to the right had slid closed when the alarm began. As he looked around the room, Hayden decided to enter the doors to the left that were still open.

The red lights continued to flood the surrounding rooms, pulsing brighter and then fading slightly in a repeating pattern. Hayden made his way down a corridor and came to another closed door. As this door hissed open in front of him, he saw a large room filled with machinery and control panels. The far side of the room was lined with windows through which the expanse of space was visible.

As Hayden stepped into the room and looked to his right, he saw a table enclosed in glass. Upon the surface of the table lay Kali. She was unconscious. Her body was nude except for two strips of white cloth that covered her chest and groin. The small monitor affixed to the side of the enclosure beeped and displayed some collection of data in a language that Hayden did not recognize. He slowly walked toward the table.

"I was beginning to think that you would never arrive," a familiar voice taunted from a corner of the room out of Hayden's sight.

Once again, Hayden's muscles tensed as he entered a defensive stance. His right palm crackled with a surge of electricity as he readied himself for the battle that he had played out over and over again inside the dreamscape. The Alva'ci emerged from behind a sizable metallic partition.

"Whatever you prepared yourself for, you are not ready for what is to come," the creature threatened.

Hayden grabbed the amulet with his left hand, and it began to glow furiously.

"The shard of my home world's sacred stone. You still

have it. You've changed it."

"Let's get this over with," Hayden demanded.

"Yes, you've come here with a goal in mind. Yet your singular purpose is but folly."

"Enough!" Hayden raised his right palm, and a bolt of lightning hurtled toward the Alva'ci.

The creature managed to deflect some of the incoming attack, and electricity bounced about the room before dissipating. However, Hayden noticed that, unlike his previous encounters with the Alva'ci, it had not managed to entirely withstand the blast.

"You shouldn't have come here," the creature's voice uttered, though noticeably weakened.

The Alva'ci fired off a retaliatory blast of energy. While still clutching the amulet with his left hand, Hayden absorbed the approaching beam of energy with his right.

"Your power has grown since we last met," the Alva'ci admitted. "You'll need it."

Hayden was slightly confused. He wondered how the Alva'ci had not recovered its strength in all the time that had passed since their last encounter. Admittedly, Hayden and the other agents of fate had triumphed in the battle on Mono Lake, but even at the end of that fight, the Alva'ci seemed more powerful than it was now. Hayden concluded that perhaps he was overthinking it. After all, he had relentlessly trained and, as the creature admitted, grown in power.

In a fantastic display of intensity, Hayden raised both of his arms and pointed his palms toward the Alva'ci. The amulet pulsed with energy around his neck. A wave of fire, lightning, and energy encased in threads of darkness from his hands tore through the air. For the first few moments, the Alva'ci deflected the blast, sending ricochets of energy throughout the room. As its strength faltered, the attack finally landed with devastating consequences.

The Alva'ci fell to the floor, its body ravaged from Hayden's blast. In the background noise of the room, Hayden noticed a distinct beeping sound that had not been present before. Taking his eyes off his opponent, Hayden looked back to see the glass enclosure around Kali retracting down into the table. Hayden's hopeful gaze was quickly interrupted by another sound in the room, and his attention was drawn away from Kali.

A growing hiss, accompanied by the noise of occasional cracking, echoed through the room from several locations. The part of Hayden's attack that the Alva'ci had managed to deflect had damaged the structure. The windows lining the front of the room showed obvious damage, and small pits in the walls were beginning to slowly grow into holes.

The Alva'ci struggled to its knees and hobbled to a nearby panel filled with buttons and gauges. In its final expenditure of strength, the creature slammed its fist against a large yellow button on the middle of the panel. As the Alva'ci collapsed back onto the floor, the doors leading out of the room slammed closed, and a set of heavy-duty blast doors descended over them. Sounds of machinery whirring to life filled the air.

"You fool," the Alva'ci uttered, hurling one last insult at Hayden.

Kali opened her eyes and began to sit up. Through the fogginess of her newly regained consciousness, she looked over at Hayden as he ran toward her.

"Hayden! What…"

Her question was abruptly cut short as the hull of the structure gave way to the damage and tore apart. Hayden leapt and grabbed Kali as the walls and floor disintegrated around him and littered the surrounding expanse of space.

عاصفة

Chapter Two

Homecoming

Hayden clung to Kali and looked back at the structure. The room that they had been in was completely gone, nothing more than pieces floating in space. The rest of the structure was still intact.

As they drifted in space near the wreckage, Hayden's mind alerted him of the danger. However, he quickly noticed that both he and Kali were okay, even though he had not activated a forcefield around them. He was surprised to learn that Armond's earlier suggestion was actually unnecessary and that his powers were automatically protecting them.

The body of the Alva'ci floated about twenty-five feet in front of Hayden. It appeared that whatever it had done with activating the control panel button was indeed its last act of life. Hayden watched in amazement as the body of the

Alva'ci began to disintegrate before him.

"Finally," Kali joyously announced, her voice and body now much more alive and composed.

Hayden released Kali from his grip and let her float beside him. He took a moment to process the fact that she was there with him. At last, he had rescued her and could bring her home. They could get back to a normal life and continue the burgeoning relationship they had just restarted before pandemonium had struck Earth. After the stream of victorious thoughts filtered through his mind, Hayden came back to the reality of the moment. He noticed for the first time that Kali was now nude. The scraps of fabric that had been covering her inside the structure had apparently blown away with the other contents of the room.

Hayden reached down at the hem of his shirt to remove it and give it to Kali. His action was interrupted by a bright flash of light from the Alva'ci's rapidly disappearing body. The orange light pulsed, increasing in intensity as the last of the creature's body turned to dust. As it grew near blinding, the light began to separate into threads of swirling energy. It circled in the shape of a sphere and grew in diameter. Hayden's eyes widened as he took in the spectacle before him, uncertain of what was coming next.

The sphere of energy slowed its expansion and then

suddenly collapsed back on itself. Before Hayden had time to process what was occurring, the energy beamed toward him. The amulet began to shake around his neck as the beam made impact with him. Hayden was astonished that the amulet seemed to be absorbing the strange force.

Hayden was equally shocked when Kali stepped in front of him. The blast of energy hit her as she presumably attempted to protect him. Hayden grabbed Kali and flung her away from the beam. The amulet continued to absorb the energy as before until it finally dissipated.

"I'm sorry that I kind of forcefully moved you out of the way," Hayden said apologetically. "That beam of energy wasn't hurting me though and I didn't want you to get hurt."

"It's okay. I'm okay," Kali insisted.

Hayden drew in a deep breath and released it as he thought about everything that had just happened. As he looked over at Kali he suddenly recalled what he had been doing before the strange eruption of energy. Hayden took his shirt off and handed it to her. As Kali pulled it on, Hayden noticed that it did little to cover the lower half of her body.

"It'll do for now. We'll be going straight home anyway."

"Wait, so how exactly did you get here?" Kali questioned. "We're somewhere in space, aren't we? You couldn't have flown all the way here, right?"

"Yeah, we're a long way from home. It's a long story, so I'll just show you."

Hayden felt the amulet begin to vibrate subtly as it started to faintly glow. He placed his hand around it and felt a rush of new power flow through his body. Hayden didn't know why he was so surprised. It made sense that the amulet absorbing all of that energy would strengthen it.

"What is that thing on your necklace?"

Hayden looked down at the amulet and then back at Kali. He remembered that she hadn't seen it before in this form.

"Do you remember that shard of orange rock that was in my side? After the Alva'ci took you, the shard fell out and Abby and I figured out how to shape it into something that would help amplify my powers."

Kali stared at the amulet intently as if she were mesmerized by its glow. "Wow, it sounds like a lot has happened since I've been gone. How long has it been anyway?"

Hayden sighed. "It's been seven months."

Kali looked out into space as she bit her lower lip. She took a moment to process the information that Hayden had just told her.

"I'm sorry, babe. I would've come sooner if I had been

able to. It took way too long for us to find you and then figure out how to reach you."

"No, don't be sorry," Kali recomposed herself. "It just doesn't feel like I've been gone for seven months. To be honest, I'm amazed that you're even here. Even with all the powers you have, I still can't comprehend how you made it here."

"Oh yeah, I was going to show you that before the amulet started freaking out," Hayden replied. "Here's how I made it out here and how we're getting back."

Hayden held his right hand steady out in front of himself. The amulet began to glow more brightly and a portal opened up ten feet in front of him. Kali looked at him with slight bewilderment written on her face. The only other time she had seen a portal open was when the Alva'ci had kidnapped her.

"Let's go home," Hayden said with a renewed tone of hope in his voice.

"I can't wait to."

Hayden put his arm around Kali and held her close. With her chest pressed against his, Hayden could feel that Kali's breathing had deepened in anticipation. He flew headfirst into the portal and it snapped shut behind them.

ca ca ca ca ca ca

JANUARY 27 - 1:30 a.m.

A sudden gust of wind swept through Hayden's room and woke Abby into a frightened state. She sprung up into a sitting position on the bed and clenched at the comforter as her gaze darted around the darkened bedroom. Abby began to relax again once she saw that nothing was out of place. Her peace was short-lived.

A bright flash of light filled the room as a portal erupted forth in the center of it. Blazing hues of orange danced along the walls of the bedroom. Moments later, Hayden and Kali tumbled forth onto the bedroom floor. Abby was too stunned to move or speak at the sudden appearance of her friends.

Hayden rose to his feet and took Kali by the hand to help her up. The portal disappeared just as quickly as it had come and the room was plunged back into darkness. Hayden held his hand up and a ball of light floated from it toward the ceiling, illuminating the room once again. As Hayden walked to the dresser and rummaged through a drawer, Kali looked around the room until she ultimately locked eyes with Abby.

"Umm..." Abby stammered, realizing that Kali was

more than likely wondering what she was doing in their bed. "I'll go wake the others up. Dan is sleeping in the living room and Armond is in the guest room. We all stayed the night so we could be here when you got back."

As she stood from the bed, Abby hoped that the explanation she gave would suffice to curb any wayward suspicions that Kali was feeling. Abby raised her lips into a meek smile as a hopeful gesture. Kali took her gaze away from Abby and once again scanned the room that she had been away from for seven months. As Hayden closed the dresser drawer, Abby noticed that Kali was wearing the shirt Hayden had left in and she was nude from the waist down.

"Here's some shorts babe," Hayden said as he tossed Kali a pair of her baby-blue cotton pajama shorts. They definitely clashed with the shirt she was wearing, but Hayden figured it wasn't that big of a deal in light of things. Kali caught the shorts and slid them up over her hips.

"Relax, Abby," Hayden finally chimed in and then directed his words to Kali. "I told Dan, Armond, and Abby they could stay here until I got back… until we got back."

Kali finally broke a smile. "Don't worry, I believe you, Abby. Besides, if Hayden had moved on to another girl then why would he bring me back?"

"That's a good point," Abby replied and joined Kali in

a brief laugh at the moment of awkwardness.

Hayden shook his head as he walked to the closet and pulled out a t-shirt. "What a unique way to come back to Earth," he said as he pulled the shirt on and chuckled to himself.

A knock at the bedroom door was followed by Dan's voice speaking from the other side. "Hey Abby, are you okay in there? A loud ass noise woke me up and it sounded like it came from down here."

Hayden walked over to the door and flung it open. Dan took a step back in surprise, paused for a moment, and then grabbed Hayden in a hug.

"Good to have you back, buddy."

Dan looked up and released Hayden from the hug as soon as he saw Kali standing across the room. He ran over to Kali and embraced her, letting the reality of her being back slowly sink in. Armond appeared in the doorway with a look of amusement on his face at Dan's enthusiastic response. He gave Hayden a quick hug and then walked across the room to where Dan was still holding Kali captive in his welcome-back embrace.

"Sorry, was that a little much?" Dan asked. "I'm just happy to see you guys."

Armond took Kali's hand and bowed his head slightly.

"It is good to have you back."

"Thank you everyone," Kali addressed the room full of friends. "I'm really grateful that you never gave up hope."

"Everyone definitely played a part in making it possible to get you back home," Hayden told Kali. "Now, I don't know about everyone else, but I am starving."

"Yes, me too," Kali agreed.

Hayden led the group down the hallway to the front room. The ball of light that was illuminating the bedroom flickered out as they departed.

෫෬ ෫෬ ෫෬ ෫෬ ෫෬ ෫෬

The next morning, everyone gathered at Armond's house. He had wanted to make everyone a celebratory breakfast, but Hayden had apparently neglected to keep his kitchen well-stocked in the past couple of weeks so the group relocated. As a savory stream of smells wafted from the kitchen into the front room, amplifying everyone's hunger, the group discussed the particulars of Kali's disappearance and captivity. Armond listened in from the kitchen counter as he finished preparations to serve the morning meal.

"So what do you remember?" Abby asked Kali.

"Not much. I remember waiting on the front lawn

with you guys and then the Alva'ci appearing right as Hayden came back. I remember getting pulled into that portal."

"Anything after that?" Dan continued questioning her.

"Barely anything. I recall being on the ship. The Alva'ci strapped me down to a table. The last thing I can remember is the sound of a machine starting up and then it all went black."

Abby and Dan listened with a mixture of shock and inquisitiveness in their demeanor. Armond continued to focus on Kali's story while he began distributing plates of food to everyone.

"Hey Hayden, for someone who just won a huge victory you sure don't look like it," Dan prodded, referencing Hayden's slouched position on the couch.

"Of course I'm happy," Hayden replied. "I just can't get over the fact that it was almost too easy."

"What do you mean?" Armond finally chimed in.

"I spent all that time in the past few months training to become more powerful. But when the battle with the Alva'ci actually happened, it was nowhere near as difficult as I thought it would be."

"Well, you did get a lot stronger Hayden," Abby offered. "Maybe you were over prepared and so it seemed more simple than it was."

"I don't know. It's like the creature never regained any

of its strength back after the fight in Mono Lake. After seven months, you would assume that it would recover… not grow weaker. If I had known that, I would have gone to save Kali right after I got the portals stable."

"You came at the perfect time, because everything worked out just right," Kali reassured him.

"Yeah, let's all just be glad that you guys both made it back alive and safe," Dan reminded them.

"…and that the threat is finally gone," Armond continued. "We can live in peace again. You can all go back to leading a normal life."

As the group ate their breakfast, they continued to discuss the nuances of Kali's rescue.

🙢 🙢 🙢 🙢 🙢 🙢

As the sun set on Kali's first full day back on Earth, she and Hayden attempted to fall back into the life that they had begun seven months earlier. Kali slipped into the shower as Hayden cooked dinner. She enjoyed the feeling of the hot water running down her body and the steam awakening her senses. She cherished the lush feeling of lathering soap over her body, a luxury that she had apparently come to take for granted.

"It feels good to be back," Kali told herself. The soap suds streamed down the curves of her body to the shower floor, like the currents of a river finding their way to the ocean. Kali focused on the warmth of the water soothing her aching muscles. While she shaved her body, she took a mental inventory of all the bruises, scrapes, and scars that she had accumulated during her time off-planet.

As Kali turned off the shower, the smell of flowery body wash was replaced with the aroma of garlic, onion, and ginger seeping in from the kitchen through the partially open bathroom door. Hayden's cooking was definitely a smell that she missed. Kali patted her body and hair dry as she stared at herself in the mirror. She hung the towel up and departed for the bedroom to get dressed in her pajamas. As she walked down the hallway toward the room, Kali heard Hayden playfully whistle at her. Obviously, he had caught a brief glimpse of her nude body as she left the bathroom.

"You act like you haven't seen me in seven months!" Kali laughed and called out to him as she continued making her way to the bedroom.

"Dinner's ready!" Hayden replied.

Kali grabbed her pajama shorts and shirt from the bed and pulled them on, forgoing undergarments in the name of comfort. She appeared in the dining room just as Hayden was placing dinner on the table. On the plates sat a bed of rice topped with a sweet-and-spicy chicken stir-fry. A glass of white wine accompanied each plate. Kali sat down and let the appetizing smell fill her nostrils once again.

"This looks delicious," she told Hayden. "I don't know what I've missed the most, but your cooking is definitely up there on the list."

Hayden smirked at her and took his seat. "Well, I figured that I would prepare one of my most critically acclaimed dishes to mark the occasion," Hayden replied jokingly with a faux-posh accent.

The duo polished off the meal in record time. Kali opened a second bottle of wine while Hayden washed the dishes. She steadily sipped on the fuller-than-average glass she had poured for herself.

"Ready for some relaxation time?" Hayden asked her.

"I am," she confirmed. "I know I've basically been asleep for over a half a year, but our bed still sounds so inviting."

Hayden finished neatly stacking the plates back in the cupboard and accompanied Kali down to the bedroom. She sprawled out on the bed, enjoying the feeling as she sunk into the memory-foam topper.

"I'm going to shower real quick," Hayden told her as

he started to undress.

Kali mimicked Hayden's earlier whistle at her as he walked across the room to deposit his clothes in the laundry basket.

"Are you mocking me?" he playfully inquired.

"Never!" she joked. "Merely admiring the scenery."

Hayden laughed as he walked over to the bathroom and started up the shower. Kali flicked through television channels as she listened to the sounds of Hayden humming a song in the background as he washed himself.

For being so out of the loop on recent television shows, Kali found herself unsatisfied with any of the available choices. She continued to mercilessly click through channel after channel until Hayden once again walked into the bedroom. Kali watched as he ran the towel over his head and then draped it over the back of the desk chair to dry. She scooted over on the bed as he walked up so that he could lay next to her. As Hayden made his way onto the bed, Kali ran her hand through his still-damp hair.

"I can't find anything worth watching," she admitted as she clicked the off button on the television remote with her other hand.

"That's alright," Hayden replied. "I've been so busy training and studying the last few months that I don't think

I've watched more than a couple hours worth of shows."

"I think I'm a little overdressed," Kali joked as she looked down at her pajamas and then over at Hayden, who hadn't put on any clothes after his shower.

"True. What a fashion emergency," Hayden joked back.

Kali stood up on the bed and faked a look of surprise as she pulled her shirt over her head and tossed it on the floor. Hayden chuckled at her amusing display of flirtation, but his gaze remained fixated on her nonetheless. Kali continued her exaggerated teasing and pursed her lips in mock-suspense while her fingers pushed her shorts over her hips. Gravity pulled them down to the mattress and Kali kicked them from her ankles. As she sat atop Hayden, he looked over her body. For the first time since they had arrived back on Earth, he noticed the generous littering of cuts, bruises, and abrasions on her body.

"You definitely got a little beat up on that ship," he said. "A lot of these bruises look fresh."

"Probably from when the place basically exploded," Kali replied.

"Yeah, that makes sense," Hayden's voice trailed off as he continued examining her.

Kali watched Hayden's eyes as they ran up and

down her body, thoroughly looking for anything out of the ordinary.

"A couple small puncture-mark scars," Hayden remarked as he ran his hand lightly over her forearm.

"I assume it was from some sort of intravenous system to give me nutrition and fluids," Kali speculated.

"You're probably right," Hayden acquiesced and returned to his informal examination. He ran his hand over her chest and down her sides tracing his fingers along several small scars. Hayden ultimately stopped his trailing fingers on her lower abdomen, marking the spot of three more small scars… one just below her belly-button and the other two toward each hip and slightly lower.

"Do you know what all these scars are from?" Hayden questioned, his voice now more concerned than inquisitive.

"No," Kali answered. "I'm guessing that creature was experimenting on me while I was unconscious. I don't feel weird or anything though."

Hayden pondered silently for a few moments while looking more intently at each scar.

"Am I okay, Doctor de Vere?" Kali half-joked in an attempt to lighten the mood.

"Sorry," Hayden replied as he realized that he had turned the atmosphere much more serious than it had been.

"If you're alright with it, can I take you over to the clinic where I did my internship tomorrow? They'll let me use their equipment to do a quick x-ray and some ultrasounds. Just to make sure everything is okay."

"Oh, so you really do want to play doctor?"

Hayden finally laughed at Kali's insinuating deflection of his question.

"I'm okay with that," she finally relented after Hayden's laugh trailed off. "I'm not going to pass up some free health care."

"Okay, good," Hayden said.

"Now let's dial down the seriousness and get back to what I was trying to do," Kali said in a mockingly serious tone while she locked eyes with Hayden.

"Yes ma'am…" Hayden's voice faltered as he attempted to joke back, brazenly interrupted by Kali repositioning herself to the effect of initiating intercourse.

"It's been so long, I may have forgotten how to do this," Kali jested, her voice wavering and cracking.

Hayden breathed in sharply. "No, you haven't."

ભ ભ ભ ભ ભ ભ

Hayden awoke the next morning from the exhaustion

onset slumber that he and Kali had fallen into several hours prior. The comforter was bunched up at the foot of the bed, a testament to the abruptness with which they had fallen asleep. As he stood and walked toward the bathroom, Hayden looked back to see Kali laying on her stomach, still asleep, with her bare body sprawled chaotically out atop the mattress. He smiled at the sight as he continued into the bathroom and started the shower.

Kali woke to the scent of a floral medley filling the room. "Hayden is using my body wash," she thought to herself, as she rolled over onto her back and rubbed her eyes. The sounds of water splashing about filled the background and clouds of steam billowed forth from the open door before disappearing into the dimly-lit expanse of the bedroom. Kali yawned and opened her eyes widely in an attempt to finish waking up. She turned her head to the side and noticed Hayden's nightstand.

The amulet that Hayden wore sat atop the wood, next to the lamp. Kali stared at it for a few moments, intrigued, before sitting up. As she moved over to the edge of the bed, she maintained her gaze on the pendant. As Kali reached out her hand toward the amulet she heard the shower turn off. She withdrew her extended arm, stood up, and ventured over to the bathroom door.

"Good morning," Hayden greeted her with a smile as he opened the shower door.

"Hey, you," Kali replied and let out a deep breath. "We must have just passed out last night."

Hayden nodded his head in agreement while he moved in front of the mirror. "Pancakes? I'll make them while you shower."

"Yes, please. I am starving," Kali replied as she wrapped her arms around Hayden from behind and rested her cheek on his back.

Hayden reached a hand back and grasped Kali's bare hip to symbolically return the embrace, while he used his other hand to work his toothbrush across his teeth. Kali released her hug and stepped into the shower, hopeful that the water would still be warm as she turned it on. She let out a satisfying sigh as the warmth washed over her.

"I noticed you smell like flowers this morning," Kali peeked her head out of the shower door and teased Hayden.

"You like it?" he answered sarcastically. "I completely forgot that I used the last of my body wash last night."

"Yeah, it smells nice, right?" Kali said as she cracked open the lid of the body wash and began to lather her body.

"It does," Hayden replied. "I'm going to start making those pancakes now so they're ready when you get out."

"Thank you!"

Hayden walked into the bedroom and pulled on a pair of dark green underwear before heading down the hall to fire up the stove. As he mixed the batter and began flipping pancakes, his mind wandered back to space. He recalled his footsteps through the ship and realized that there had been doors opposite of the chamber that held Kali and the Alva'ci. For a moment, he wondered what was on the other side. His curiosity disappeared when Kali entered the room. Unintentionally, she had mirrored Hayden's choice in minimal clothing for the morning.

"Hey we just about match," Hayden joked in reference to her pair of light green panties. "Mine don't have little flowers all over them though."

"Your loss," she joked back.

Hayden sat a plate full of syrup-drenched pancakes in front of Kali. "You're lucky I didn't make fajitas for breakfast… you might have regretted going topless."

"First of all, when have you ever made fajitas for breakfast?" Kali retorted. "…and secondly, I'm like ninety-five percent sure that I'll probably end up with an ungodly amount of syrup on my chest. Though admittedly, that is better than scalding hot vegetable oil."

After breakfast, Kali and Hayden begrudgingly added

to their outfits so they could wander out into public. "Can I drive?" Kali asked Hayden as they made their way toward his car. "Everything feels like I'm doing it for the first time again."

"Yeah, of course," Hayden agreed and handed her the keys.

As they drove down the 55 freeway into Costa Mesa, Kali spotted one of the bars along Newport Boulevard that they had frequented together before she had left. "Damn, we had a lot of fun there."

"Indeed we did," Hayden agreed. "Seems like so long ago now."

Hayden interrupted the moment of reminiscing to direct Kali to make a left turn on Seventeenth Street. A couple minutes later, they pulled into a parking spot at the medical office that Hayden had completed his fall semester internship at. As they walked in, the young woman at the front desk noticed them.

"Hayden!" she said excitedly. "How's our favorite pre-med student doing? What brings you back here?"

"Hey Olivia," he replied as they approached the desk. "I need to use a room for like half an hour."

"Okay, no problem. Exam room eleven is free," she said as she buzzed Hayden and Kali through the locked door from the waiting room to the back.

"So they're just cool with you coming down here and using their offices and equipment?" Kali asked.

"What can I say, they like me here," Hayden joked. "Oh, and my mother went to college with the head physician, so that helps too."

"Okay, now that explains it."

Hayden led Kali into the exam room and tossed her a cloth gown from the cupboard.

"Really?" she asked.

"Hey, they're pretty luxurious gowns," Hayden replied. "I mean, I obviously don't care if you don't wear anything, I just wanted you to have it available in case someone knocked on the door."

"True, I guess. I'll keep it next to me."

Kali undressed herself and sat on the exam table while Hayden pulled an ultrasound machine over and flicked it on.

"Oh, I know what that attachment is for," Kali said as Hayden set the first of two probes on the tray next to him.

Hayden smirked as he continued preparing. "Yeah, we're going to be looking at a little of everything."

Kali settled back on the exam table as Hayden began imaging all the areas of her body that had incision scarring. Once he was completed with the ultrasounds, Hayden ran chest, abdominal, and pelvic x-ray's on her.

"So, what's the verdict?" Kali asked him as they went back into the exam room.

"Well, there's nothing abnormal," Hayden replied. "Obviously, that doesn't mean that the Alva'ci didn't experiment on you or something… but it didn't implant anything in you or take any organs."

"Well, thank God for that," Kali let out a sigh of relief.

ɐɔ ɐɔ ɐɔ ɐɔ ɐɔ ɐɔ

A week passed and Hayden felt a growing sense of peace coming back into his life. As he lay in bed, Hayden looked over at Kali and watched her chest rise and fall with each breath as she slept. Hayden kept his gaze fixated on her until he too drifted off to sleep.

Just before dawn, Kali awoke and carefully rose from the bed. She walked over near Hayden's nightstand and stared at the amulet as it sat idly on the wood. After a minute, Hayden stirred and opened his eyes.

"Hey, good morning. What are you doing?" he asked Kali.

"Oh, nothing. I went to the bathroom and was just about to come back to bed. Was looking at your little pendant thing."

"Well come back to bed for a couple more hours," Hayden replied. "It's too early to get up already."

"Can I hold it?" Kali asked in reference to the amulet, as she reached her hand down toward it.

"No, you shouldn't touch it," Hayden told her, now more awake. "I don't know what would happen to someone that doesn't have my powers if they held it. It could be very dangerous."

"You really aren't going to let me just touch it?"

"Kali, it could hurt you. It may even kill you to touch it."

"Whatever, Hayden," Kali snapped back.

"Babe, it's not that big of a deal," Hayden replied. "I just don't want you to get hurt."

Kali walked over to the dresser and rifled through a drawer. She maintained her silence as she pulled on underwear and pants.

"What are you doing?" Hayden asked.

Kali put on a bra and pulled a shirt over her head. "I'm leaving! You're being an asshole."

"Wait... what?"

Kali turned and walked out of the bedroom. As Hayden pulled himself out of bed and quickly dressed himself in a pair of nearby pajama shorts, he heard the front door open and close. Hayden rushed down the hallway. As he walked outside onto the front lawn, Kali was nowhere to be seen. He pulled his phone out and dialed Abby.

"Hello?" Abby muttered, obviously still mostly asleep. "What time is it? Is something wrong?"

"Yeah, Kali just freaked out and took off walking. I was like ten seconds behind her coming out of the apartment, but I didn't see her anywhere."

"What happened?" Abby asked.

"She had apparently got up to go to the bathroom. I woke up to see her standing by the bed. She was looking down at the amulet and then she asked if she could hold it. I told her it was way too dangerous and then she got all mad and took off."

"That's really odd," Abby admitted. "I'll jump in my car and head over to you. Maybe I'll see her walking."

"Okay, thanks Abby. I'm going to look some more, but I'll be here when you arrive."

Hayden hung up the phone and ascended into the air. As he climbed a few hundred feet up, he used the enhanced point of view to look for anyone walking in the area. To his dismay, he saw no one. Once he saw Abby's car approaching, he landed back on his driveway to greet her.

"Anything?" he asked as Abby exited her car.

"Nope," Abby replied. "Her phone is going straight to voicemail also."

Hayden and Abby went inside to wait and brainstorm ideas of where Kali could have possibly walked to so quickly. They called Dan and Armond to make sure that Kali hadn't shown up to either of their homes.

"It's like she disappeared," Hayden mused.

"So, this might sound a little invasive," Abby started. "But can't you use the amulet to find her presence? Like you did when you were searching all those planets?"

"You're right, on both accounts," Hayden replied. "I could do that… and yeah, that's a little stalkerish given the circumstances."

"Okay, yeah I know it's not ideal," Abby admitted. "I just think you should do it to make sure that she's safe. Like make sure that no one saw her walking and threw her in the back of a van. I'm not saying that you should find her and then show up where she's at."

Hayden reluctantly stood up. "I suppose… to make sure she's safe. Let me go grab it."

A few moments later, Hayden came back down the hallway with the amulet in hand. As he closed his eyes, the stone began to glow. Abby scooted up to the edge of the couch cushion in anticipation. When Hayden finally opened his eyes, Abby's look changed from intent focus to impatient inquisitiveness.

"So?" she asked, noticing Hayden's perplexed expression.

"She's not… anywhere."

بدون

Chapter Three

The Abassilon Prophecy

Later that night, Hayden decided to go on a drive. Kali had yet to show up, and none of the group had heard from her. Hayden's mind constantly bounced back and forth between possible explanations, but he couldn't settle on any that made sense. Her reaction earlier that morning was puzzling.

Hayden arrived in Los Angeles and jumped off the 101 onto Cahuenga Boulevard, eventually making his way up to an overlook on Mulholland Drive that he had previously taken Kali to. He pulled over and sat on the trunk of his car. As he looked out over the city, Hayden contemplated the past year. He had lost one of his best friends, Kali had come back and rekindled their relationship, and his life was upended by a random stroke of destiny. After all that he had gone through to get Kali back, Hayden was baffled by her sudden fit of anger in what he deemed a trivial moment. A moment in which he was looking out for her safety. They had been so content and amicable up until that point. He felt alone.

A couple hours passed, and Hayden finally decided to head back home. He had processed his thoughts as much as possible and would resume the search for Kali in the morning. He secretly hoped that she would be waiting for him back at the apartment when he arrived. Luckily, the freeways back to Fullerton were mostly empty.

ↄ ↄ ↄ ↄ ↄ ↄ

The alarm jolted Hayden from an otherwise peaceful sleep. He looked over at his phone and confirmed the time: nine o'clock in the morning. Hayden quickly readied himself with a shower and a light breakfast. He settled onto the couch and closed his eyes to search for Kali's presence once again. He concentrated for several minutes and was confronted with the same result as the day before. There was no trace of Kali's presence anywhere. He began to worry that something nefarious had occurred.

As Hayden opened his eyes, he was startled to find that the glow of the amulet had slightly changed hues from orange to a deep green color. As he examined the stone, the color quickly changed back, and then the glow faded away altogether.

"That's really weird," Hayden said aloud to himself. He put the amulet down on the coffee table. Though he was curious about the cause of the impromptu color change, he decided that he didn't need another distraction at the moment.

Hayden called Abby, Dan, and Armond to check in with them and make sure no one else had heard from Kali. He knew they would have, of course, contacted him if they had heard anything. The calls were nothing more than an exercise in futility meant to occupy idle time, a desperate hope for some fluke. Abby and Dan both offered to come over and keep Hayden company. He accepted their offers and decided to clean the apartment while waiting.

Beginning in the bedroom, Hayden gathered clothes and placed them in the laundry basket, tidied up the nightstands and desk, and made the bed. Hayden rummaged through the basket full of clean clothes that he and Kali had neglected to put away for the last two days. As he filled the dresser drawers, Hayden stopped abruptly when he thought he heard the front door open. A moment later, he was certain it had actually happened when he heard the door close. He placed the remaining mix of underwear that was in his hand on top of the dresser and proceeded cautiously down the hallway.

"Hey babe," Kali called out from the kitchen when Hayden appeared.

Hayden was taken aback by her distinctly casual tone. Her voice and mannerisms made it appear as if she had just gone down the street for a few minutes to grab some breakfast... not that she had been gone without a trace or adequate explanation for an entire day.

"Hi," Hayden replied, taking a moment to collect his thoughts. "What happened yesterday?"

"I'm sorry. I know that I freaked out and was way too upset about nothing. I guess I've just been really stressed, but I know it doesn't really excuse my behavior."

"I looked for you and couldn't find you anywhere," Hayden continued. "I'm not going to demand you tell me where you were or anything, but I was at a complete loss for an explanation or a clue where you could be."

"I went to the beach," Kali offered. "I got a rideshare car to meet me down the street and just spent the time thinking."

"You spent the night at the beach?" Hayden asked, genuinely confused.

Before Kali could answer, there was a knock at the door.

"Oh, that's going to be Abby and Dan. They were coming over to keep me company."

"We should all go out to eat lunch!" Kali suggested excitedly as Abby and Dan entered the room. "I need to take a shower really quick, but after that, let's all go."

Hayden glanced over at their friends, and they all exchanged confused looks at Kali's behavior.

"You guys, I'm fine!" Kali insisted as she sensed the awkwardness filling the room. "I overreacted, and I hope you all can forgive me… but everything is okay."

"Okay, yeah, jump in the shower babe. Then we'll all head out for lunch," Hayden relented.

Kali walked down the hall toward the bedroom. Hayden, Abby, and Dan remained silent until they heard the shower come on.

"What?" Dan said in disbelief.

"I don't even know," Hayden admitted. "She says she caught a ride to the beach and spent the night there thinking. She apologized, and that was that. I guess I'm just shocked because it seems like nothing even happened to her."

"Dude…" Dan said in a tone that suggested his next words may be controversial. "Can't you run down to the room real quick and check her phone apps to see if she actually ordered a ride?"

"I'm not going to that," Hayden predictably resisted. "I'll take her at her word and see how the rest of the day plays out. If everything is good and back to normal, then I'm just glad she's safe and back home."

"I think that's the perfect way to go on this," Abby added.

The trio moved to the front room and waited for Kali to finish getting ready. As they sat, Hayden recalled the strange occurrence from earlier.

"Oh, I almost completely forgot. Something weird happened this morning," Hayden told Abby and Dan. "The amulet changed colors. It was glowing green for like a minute, and then it changed back to orange."

"What does that mean?" Abby asked.

"I have no clue," Hayden answered. "Honestly, I'm too preoccupied to even think about it right now. That mystery can wait for another day. I'm sure Armond will know something."

"So, Eduardo Quesada's?" Kali asked cheerfully as she appeared at the end of the hallway. "I'm craving some enchiladas right now."

ↄ ↄ ↄ ↄ ↄ ↄ

Later that night, Kali continued to apologize for her behavior and seductively enticed Hayden to forget about the entire ordeal. Afterward, sleep came quickly.

Hayden found himself in an incredibly vivid and lifelike dream. It almost felt like he was within the dreamscape with the levels of clarity and realism he experienced. When he woke in the morning, Hayden felt as if he had only slept a few minutes. At the same time, he felt that the dream had lasted for hours.

The entire group met at Armond's home in the afternoon for lunch and a discussion about what was to come. Armond was debating whether or not it was the right time for him to move back to New York and resume operating the bookstore that he owned with his brother. While Kali and Abby chatted on the back patio, Hayden approached Armond.

"I had a dream last night that seemed kind of pertinent, Hayden told him. "I can't really explain why it feels important to me, but it does."

"Okay, what was it?"

"I saw a girl in the distance, standing on the shore of a beach with the waves lapping at her feet as they repeated in their indefinite cresting rhythm," Hayden explained. "Her hair was flowing in the wind, the same breeze washing over my face as I walked toward her. Each step I took felt heavier than the last, the feeling inside me more impending with every stride. In the sky above her were two stars, blazing with intensity through the morning light. I reached out my hand as I approached her, but I woke up before she turned around to face me."

Armond pulled a book from the nearby shelf, its cover undeniably testifying to its antiquity. He rifled through the pages intently before stopping and placing the open book on the table in front of Hayden. Armond pointed to a passage, and Hayden read it meticulously in his head.

"The Abassilon Prophecy," Armond said once he could tell that Hayden had completed reading.

"So why did I dream that?"

"Your guess is as good as mine," Armond replied. "Honestly, that prophecy is the least understood one of them all. Over the years, everyone has pretty much ignored it because it doesn't have any relevance to the mission of the agents of fate. It is vague in who it speaks about. I would postulate that it's merely a brief story between the cognizant one and someone significant in their life."

Hayden thought in silence for a moment. "That makes

sense, I suppose. Even though I couldn't actually see who the girl was, I could see that her hair was blonde. So if that's what the prophecy is about, then Kali fits that description."

"Very true. But try not to dwell on it too much."

"Alright, thank you," Hayden said. "I guess that makes me feel better after everything that has happened in the last few days."

"Well, you and Kali definitely deserve some peace and quiet for a change."

"Oh, that reminds me," Hayden changed the subject. "My amulet was very briefly glowing green instead of orange yesterday. What does that mean?"

Armond began to speak but audibly faltered. He looked down and searched his memory for a few moments. "I hate to say this, but I do not know what it means. The amulet was never mentioned in any of the prophecies. Also, any time that the Alva'ci is mentioned, orange is the only color ever associated with it. Did anything else happen?"

"No, nothing else," Hayden replied. "It lasted for like sixty seconds and then went back to normal. It hasn't happened again since."

Armond took a heavy breath in and out. "Perhaps I shouldn't be so quick to return to New York after all."

෪ ෪ ෪ ෪ ෪ ෪

As Hayden settled into bed, he found himself restless and unable to fall asleep. The television murmured in the background, with its ever-changing pattern of light illuminating Kali's face. Hayden watched as her breathing became heavier and her eyelids sprung to life with dream-induced activity.

Finding himself daydreaming about the future, Hayden almost didn't realize the change in the room's lighting. The amulet began to glow from the nightstand with a green hue, adding its colors to those of the television. Hayden slowly rose from the bed and grabbed the amulet. Kali was still asleep.

Hayden wandered down the hallway and sat on the couch. He examined the amulet for any other changes but couldn't find any. As he watched it, the green color faded in and out. Hayden looked over at the microwave. It was one o'clock in the morning. Armond would likely be asleep.

The restlessness was beginning to wear off, and Hayden felt the call of sleep beckoning. He was finally ready to call it a night and escape into the world of his dreams.

"Dreams…" Hayden muttered aloud. "What about the dreamscape?"

Hayden clutched the amulet and closed his eyes. His body went limp, and fell back. The glow of the amulet disappeared as soon as Hayden's head hit the cushion behind him.

Darkness swirling with a light fog surrounded Hayden as he opened his eyes inside the dreamscape. There was nothing. He took a few steps forward and found himself at the edge of a vast lake. The water was as black and ominous as the void around him. Hayden looked out into the nothingness and saw a faint green light in the distance. It was pulsating as if it were a light at the end of a distant dock.

"Well, what the hell, let's do this," Hayden said to himself.

Hayden closed his eyes and concentrated. When he opened his eyes again, he was standing on the end of the dock. The green light stood before him, floating about three feet off the wooden platform. As he approached the light, it faded away. Moments later, it reappeared this time orange in color. It was the orb that he had defeated within the dreamscape last year before the battle in Mono Lake.

"How are you here?" Hayden asked the orb. "I saw your body disintegrate in space."

"That you did," the orb responded. "My body is gone. My power flowed into your amulet. Within that power, all that remains of me are my memories. Those memories, enhanced by the power of this place, are what now embody the orb."

"So you called me here by changing the color of the amulet?" Hayden asked.

"I did," the orb admitted. "You have won your battle against me. However, your war is far from over. You need to know what I know."

"What is it that you want to tell me?"

"You must have a feeling of it already," the orb taunted. "I am sure that you went back to your planet almost fearful of how simple it was to defeat me."

"Yes, it was far too easy."

"I'm sure you realized that I was not at the peak of my abilities," the orb continued. "Did you ask yourself why?"

"Of course I did," Hayden replied. "I cannot figure out why you were so much less powerful after having seven whole months to recover."

"I had recovered significantly within a month of leaving Earth," the orb told Hayden. "Then I found something that would add to my power exponentially."

"Add to your power?" Hayden questioned. "Obviously, that didn't happen."

"No," the orb replied. "When I say that I found

something, it may be better to actually say that I awakened something."

"Okay, what did you awaken?"

"Your powers were dormant within humanity for a very long time," the orb continued. "There was another power that has been dormant as well. According to what I know, many believed it to be gone entirely. As I started to experiment on Kali, I went too far for her body to endure. She flat-lined on the table."

"She died?"

"Yes, for a few minutes," the orb answered. "That's when it awakened. A purple light rose from her chest, and she came back to life. Purple signifies only one thing within the realm of the powers that humans used to possess. The power was last held by one person for thousands of years, a woman named Bilv'at. She was also called al-Dahr by the ancestors of Abbas and the others that I fought so long ago."

"So you're saying that this long-gone power was within Kali? What is it?" Hayden asked in disbelief.

"Indeed it was," the orb stated simply. "The grandfathers of Abbas and Ahjiamed had journeyed to meet with Bilv'at. They sought access to one specific use of her power. She offered to teach them if they gathered five powerful talismans and brought them to her. Although she thought it would be an impossible task, they returned to her ten years later with all five in hand. Bilv'at kept her word and taught them a spell that would access her powers for their desired use."

Hayden began pacing on the dock, the wood creaking under his footsteps. "Okay, what did they want to use her powers for?"

"Time," the orb told him. "Bilv'at held the power over time. The grandfathers of Abbas and Ahjiamed used the spell to extend their lifetimes to almost a thousand years. They still died eventually. Some died more quickly from injuries, as the spell did not make them invulnerable to harm. When I arrived on Earth, Abbas and Ahjiamed were already hundreds of years old. After our battle, Abbas cast a spell to bind me far underground. That spell also sacrificed the abilities of humans to use any of the powers, which is why they all went dormant. When the spell was cast, Bilv'at also lost her power, and she died immediately. Her power has never been seen since, and the spell vanished from memory forever."

"So Kali has this power," Hayden asked. "...over time?"

"She does," the orb replied. "I put her to sleep and attempted to capture her power so I could possess it. At least, I thought that I had put her to sleep. However, it turns out that she was very much awake. Kali began to draw power from me, which is why I was as weak as I was when you came to rescue her. You wouldn't listen to anything I had to say then."

"Well, forgive my mistrust in light of the fact that you kidnapped and tortured my girlfriend," Hayden replied snarkily. "I just wanted to finally get her back."

"I do not judge you for that," the orb responded. "However, you need to know that she isn't done. Her power is still very much awake. The power that she drew off of me was inconsequential compared to what you gained from fashioning that amulet… but she did capture much more power when she placed herself in front of you after my death. You may have been fooled into thinking she was merely trying to protect you from harm, but her intentions were sinister. You, of all people, should know that the powers of the Alva'ci race have an enormous propensity to corrupt humans who attempt to harness them. You have been the only human to ever overcome that corruption. The same cannot be said for Kali."

"I don't believe you," Hayden reacted instinctively.

"Of course, you don't want to admit this reality to yourself," the orb acquiesced. "Test what I am telling you. Bring her into the dreamscape. You'll be able to see the aura of corruptive power around her. However, once you do, prepare yourself for the consequences. Her power continues to grow, and she will use it in line with the corruption that has taken over her soul."

Hayden sighed, contemplating the dreadful possibility that the orb was telling the truth. "Fine, I will try what you are suggesting."

"You need to go," the orb urged. "Get out now!"

Hayden awoke from the dreamscape as Kali was walking into the front room.

"Hey, what are you doing out here, babe?" she asked.

"I was restless," Hayden told her, hiding the fear in his voice. "I guess I just passed out on the couch."

"Well, come back to bed," she insisted. "I miss you."

ɛ3 ɛ3 ɛ3 ɛ3 ɛ3 ɛ3

Indecisiveness ate away at Hayden's mind the following morning. He didn't want to believe what the Alva'ci had told him about Kali, but he couldn't deny the feeling that had bothered him ever since returning to Earth. Part of him wanted to ignore the issue and hope everything was fine. However, Hayden knew that he would be continually plagued with uncertainty if he followed that course.

Hayden and Kali had spent the morning relaxing. There was a sense of calm in doing nothing. As he and Kali showered together in the late morning, Hayden finally worked up the will to address the thoughts in his head.

"Babe, you remember that carnival scene that we went into before I left to fight in Mono Lake?" Hayden asked Kali as she covered herself in body wash.

"Yeah, in the dreamscape thing you can do?" Kali replied. "It was exactly like the actual carnival we went to years ago. It was pretty amazing."

"I was thinking that maybe we could have a little lunch date today," Hayden suggested. "We can go back into the dreamscape, and I can recreate the scene from when we had that picnic together at the park in Newton."

"Oh yeah? That would be beautiful," Kali agreed. "Wait, can you even eat lunch in that dreamscape place?"

"Yeah, you can eat," Hayden replied. "It's just not real food, but your mind thinks it is."

"Okay, yeah, let's do it!"

Hayden pushed through the reluctance to follow through with his plan. He felt guilty for essentially tricking Kali into this test but remained hopeful that the Alva'ci had lied to him. Hayden decided that he could forgive himself if everything ended up being okay.

Kali reached out of the shower and grabbed both towels. After drying off and getting dressed, she and Hayden went out to the front room.

"I'm ready when you are," Kali told Hayden.

They took a seat on the couch next to each other. Hayden reminded her to sit back on the cushions so she wouldn't fall off the couch when they entered the dreamscape.

"I love you," Hayden told her. "I'm so glad you're back."

"I love you too."

Hayden took her hands and told her to close her eyes. A moment later, their bodies fell back as they entered the dreamscape.

سلام

Chapter Four

Celestial Bodies

Kali and Hayden opened their eyes to find a lush expanse of grass surrounding them. Pockets of wooded areas stood on the borders of the park. A red and black plaid blanket was on the grass, neatly adorned with a picnic basket and a bottle of wine. A light breeze whipped through the trees, scented with a faint aroma of lavender. Hayden was amazed at how incredibly accurate the scene was to his memory of when he and Kali had visited the park several years ago.

They had taken the trip to Newton together to visit Paige, who was on a summer internship with a company based in Boston. As one of the perks of being selected for the highly competitive internship program, Paige was provided with accommodations at a company-owned house in the nearby city of Newton. Kali and Hayden flew out about a month into Paige's internship and spent three weeks with her. Although Paige was regularly busy with her work at the company, she spent as much time as she could in the evenings and weekends with them.

During all of the time that Paige was away at work, Hayden and Kali spent their time together. They explored the city and surrounding areas, venturing out for day trips to New York, Pennsylvania, and Rhode Island. As the weeks went on, the attraction between Kali and Hayden grew stronger. Truthfully, Hayden knew that it had already been there before the trip but had remained unspoken and trapped in a seemingly eternal infancy.

As the second week of their trip began, Hayden could tell that he and Kali were definitely getting closer. The previously subtle hints of flirtation that had been dappled throughout their friendship became much more perspicuous with each passing day. In the final week of their vacation, Hayden took Kali to a nearby carnival, where they shared their first kiss. Three days later, they set out on a picnic at the same park that now surrounded them in the dreamscape.

As Hayden drifted from his memories back into the present, he looked up at Kali. She was wearing a white embellished knee-length dress. The hem of her dress fluttered in the breeze. The guipure lace straps hung on her shoulders, and the deeply plunging neckline revealed just enough bust to momentarily distract Hayden from his purpose.

Kali smiled and took in a deep breath of the familiar aroma on the breeze. She thought of just how idyllic this moment had been for her in the past. For her, it had marked a substantial turning point in the relationship between her and Hayden. Transforming it from a friendship with romantic overtures floating just beneath the surface, into a rapidly blossoming love story bursting with intense emotion. As Kali continued to admire the scenery in the dreamscape, Hayden refocused his attention.

"You're staring at me," Kali teased him. "Do you still like this dress all these years later?"

Hayden stumbled to find words. "Yes, of course… it looks beautiful on you."

Kali noticed the peculiar look on Hayden's face as he gazed at her. She looked down at herself and immediately recognized what he was so intently looking at. Her body was surrounded by wisps of purple and orange light. Her head sprung back up, and she looked Hayden in the eyes.

"Kali, let me help you," Hayden pleaded.

Kali took several steps toward Hayden but did not

respond. She forcefully thrust the palm of her right hand into Hayden's chest. As he flew backward, the scene around him went black.

Hayden jolted awake on the couch in his living room. Kali was standing over him with her hands grasping the amulet around his neck. Blinding orange light flooded the room and spilled out the windows of the apartment.

"Give it to me, Hayden," she insisted.

Hayden stood and placed his hands on Kali's arms. "No, Kali. Let me help you. We can get through this together."

"I said give it to me!" her voice became fierce with anger.

The back of Hayden's hands began to glow with symbols of power. Electricity flowed through his body, startling Kali enough to loosen her grip on the amulet. With his right hand, Hayden hit Kali with a gust of air that sent her flying back into the wall. Even though he was holding back from the full force of his powers, Hayden was still surprised that Kali hardly seemed stunned by the blast.

"I don't need your help," Kali scolded him as she composed herself.

As she glared at Hayden, Kali took his remorse and used it to her advantage. Much to his surprise, Kali waved her hand at her side and opened a portal. The intense orange glow disappeared into nothingness as she stepped into it. Hayden fell back onto the couch, aghast, alone, and trembling with disbelief.

ↄ ↄ ↄ ↄ ↄ ↄ

Five hours later, Hayden finally dug up the willpower to pull himself from the couch. He had spent the time in thought. As he attempted to process what had happened, he found himself in a loop of relapsing into denial and disbelief. He looked over at his phone and tallied the number of missed calls. As he stood, he dialed Armond.

"I'm coming over," Hayden stated as Armond answered the phone."

"Okay…" Armond replied just before the line went dead.

A bright orange flash appeared in Armond's living room, and Hayden stepped out of a portal.

"Come on in," Armond said in an attempt at being humorous.

"Everything is fucked," Hayden replied bluntly, ignoring Armond's joke.

"What do you mean?" Armond asked, his face now swept with seriousness.

"Kali is gone," Hayden started. "The amulet started glowing green again last night. I went into the dreamscape, and the essence or memory of the Alva'ci was there. It spoke to me and warned me that Kali had a power of her own. It also said that she had been secretly leeching off of its power to grow stronger. That's why the creature was so weak when I fought it in space. It told me that her mind was corrupted. I didn't believe it, but the Alva'ci told me to bring her into the dreamscape to test what it had told me. This morning, I did that. It ended with her attacking me and trying to take the amulet. I held her off, and then she opened a portal and disappeared."

The look of shock on Armond's face said more than any words he could muster in the moment. Both Armond and Hayden stood in silence for a minute.

"I'm sorry, Hayden," Armond finally replied. "You had just gotten her back. I know this must be killing you inside."

"Yeah, it is," Hayden admitted, his voice now breaking as emotion lapped over his mind like a series of tidal waves. "I told her that I could help her... I asked her to let me help her. She just attacked me in response. The Alva'ci wasn't lying to me. Her mind has deeply embedded corruption from the creature's power. To be perfectly honest, I don't even know for sure if I would be able to help her."

"I'm at a loss," Armond said. "What are you going to do? What do you think she wants?"

"Well, I know she wants the amulet," Hayden replied. "She touched it, and it didn't harm her at all, so this power she has must be substantial. If she's after the amulet and has been corrupted, I can only imagine that her motives are sinister."

"We should warn the others," Armond suggested. "Kali may go after them to try to get to you."

"Good idea," Hayden said.

Armond called Dan while Hayden dialed Abby. After communicating the events that had transpired and the potential threat, everyone agreed to meet up at Armond's.

"I'll come get you right now," Hayden told Abby over the phone. "I'm going to open a portal into your living room to get you here as quickly as possible."

"Okay, I'm ready for you," Abby replied.

"Let Dan know that I'll come for him right after I get Abby back here," Hayden instructed Armond. "Okay, here I come, Abby."

Hayden hung up the phone and opened a portal. He stepped out of Armond's home and into Abby's apartment.

"Hi…" Abby began but was interrupted.

A second portal opened near Hayden and Abby. Kali walked into the room and immediately struck Abby, knocking her to the ground. Hayden began to react, but Kali wrapped her arms around him and pulled him into the portal with her. Abby gasped as she stumbled back to her feet and saw the portal disappear before her eyes. She quickly jumped through Hayden's still-open portal to Armond's home just before it too vanished.

Armond caught Abby as she stumbled out of the portal. As he examined the blood running down her cheek, he knew that something had gone terribly wrong.

"Kali appeared out of nowhere and took Hayden with her," Abby informed him.

Ꮞ Ꮞ Ꮞ Ꮞ Ꮞ Ꮞ

Kali released Hayden from her grasp as they fell from the portal into the expanse of space. Hayden wasn't sure exactly where they were, but a giant planet loomed in the distance, and asteroid fragments surrounded the area.

"Neat trick, wasn't it?" Kali boasted.

"How did you know that I would be at Abby's at just that moment?" Hayden questioned.

"Because I can track your portals," Kali replied. "You can't hide from me."

"Kali, please let me help you get through this," Hayden

pleaded. "I just got you back. I need us to be okay. I need this all to be over."

"Well, it looks like you were a little too late in rescuing me," Kali taunted. "I'm not interested in your help, Hayden. I just want your amulet."

"I can't give that to you," Hayden told her, exasperated.

"Alright, then I'll have to take it from you."

"Kali, don't try that. I don't want to fight you. I don't want to hurt you."

"Don't worry, babe. You won't be able to hurt me."

With her last bit of arrogant taunting, Kali unleashed her powers. She pulled two car-size asteroids from nearby and sent them hurtling toward Hayden.

"This is pointless!" Hayden yelled at Kali as he activated his powers and easily vaporized the incoming threats.

In an instant, Kali disappeared. Just as quickly, she appeared behind Hayden. He felt a forceful blow against his back.

"I'm just having fun right now," Kali yelled back as Hayden tumbled through space.

After stabilizing himself, Hayden looked back over at Kali and decided that if he was going to have any chance of helping her, he would first have to subdue her. His hands blazed with symbols of power, and his palms lit with radiating energy.

"That's more like it," Kali once again taunted him.

Hayden let out a groan of displeasure as he fired dual blasts of energy at Kali. Once again, he was still pulling his punches in fear that he would hurt her. Yet Hayden was still mildly surprised to watch Kali redirect his attack back at him. Frustrated more than anything, Hayden deflected the blast into another nearby asteroid, shattering it into tiny pieces.

As the battle continued back and forth, Hayden slowly ramped up the power of his attacks. Each time, Kali met the challenge. Hayden also found that her attacks were becoming increasingly difficult to deflect and counter.

"Why do you persist?" Kali asked him, pausing her barrage of attacks momentarily.

"You know why!" Hayden responded, with a hint of frustrated anger now evident in his voice. "I need to end this pointless conflict so that you can get better again."

"Babe, I'm better than I've ever been," Kali retorted. "Just look at me. I have unimaginable power. I thought you would be proud of me."

"Proud of you?" Hayden asked as he shook his head in disbelief at Kali's words. "If your mind hadn't been corrupted by you leeching all that power from the Alva'ci, then yeah, I would probably be ecstatic as long as you were happy. But you need help before it's too late. Not to mention the fact that you lied to me, attacked me, and tried to steal the amulet."

"Listen, Hayden," she replied. "Just give me the amulet. Once I have it, then I'll let you help me all you want."

"You actually expect me to believe that?"

"I expect you to want what's best for me… and that is letting me achieve my full potential. I know you want to be with me. We can still be together. Just let me have that amulet. I'll even give it back to you after I'm done with it."

"If you got this corrupted by the little power that you weaned off the Alva'ci, this amulet is going to irreversibly destroy your mind. I know what this thing can do. It isn't healthy."

"I'll be fine!" Kali insisted. "Just let me have it for a few moments. Then we can go back home. We'll go shower, and I'll make the rest of the night so good for you that you'll forget any of this even happened."

"Kali, if you actually cared, you would be able to see that you're killing me inside right now. You are not yourself."

"Why do I bother talking this over with you?" Kali asked as she rolled her eyes.

Hayden prepared for the inevitable incoming attack. Without fail, Kali flung a barrage of energy blasts toward Hayden. Once again, he deflected them. The two lovers turned adversaries were at a stalemate. Hayden was about to speak to her again when she struck with immense speed.

Within an instant, two flashes of light appeared near Hayden. Kali had opened two portals to either side of him. She had sucked an asteroid through the first one and fired off an enormous energy blast through the second one. In the fraction of a second that it took Hayden to think of the spell Chantiatus and bring up a forcefield to deflect the blow, the attacks landed and obliterated it. Hayden was stunned and hung on the edge of consciousness.

As Kali began to approach him in apparent victory, Hayden closed his eyes and momentarily slipped into the dreamscape. Once inside, he seared the blank canvas around himself with energy. The resulting overload jolted him back awake and prompted his body to dole out a massive dose of epinephrine, keeping him conscious. As he began to recover, Hayden grasped the amulet.

An intense white light radiated from around Hayden as he focused his energy. The symbols of power all flickered in sequence on the back of his hands as he readied himself to unleash an attack of actual substance at Kali. As she continued to approach, Kali could feel the shockwaves of pure energy emanating from Hayden as they rippled out into space.

Hayden attacked with power, unlike anything Kali had seen from him before. The colossal stream of infused energy cut through the distance between them instantly. Hayden opened his eyes, fearing that the attack had been too much and Kali would be gone.

"Good effort," she said mockingly. Floating above her left palm was an orb of the condensed energy blast that Hayden had fired at her. "It looks like we're just going to go back and forth until one of us dies of exhaustion."

The surprise that reverberated through Hayden's body visibly manifested as his hands shook involuntarily. In a snap instinctual decision, Hayden reacted by using a facet of Ane'illuminus that he previously deemed too controversial to employ.

"Run away!" Hayden used the power of Ane'illuminus to push the command into Kali's mind.

Kali's body visibly twitched and spasmed as she resisted the foreign thought taking over her mind.

"Fine," she snarled. "But enjoy your consequences."

Orange and purple wisps of energy swirled above Kali's right palm. As she pushed her hands together, all of the energy combined into a massive beam of energy. Kali fired it directly into the surface of the nearby dwarf planet Ceres. Hayden watched as the energy enveloped the sphere.

"...and here they come," taunted Kali.

Ceres exploded in a spectacular burst of energy into billions of fragments. Hayden watched as Kali opened a portal through which he recognized the sight of Earth. As Kali's willpower to resist the command that Hayden had pushed into her mind finally began to fade, she swept her hand in front of her. Thousands of the fragments of Ceres changed course and sped into the portal.

"Have fun with that," Kali said before opening another portal and vanishing.

⭕ ⭕ ⭕ ⭕ ⭕ ⭕

Hayden fought the urge swirling through his mind to break down and give up. He composed himself and flew into a portal. As he came out the other side, he floated near the Moon. In the distance, he could clearly see that some of the fragments of Ceres that Kali had sent screaming toward Earth were already pocking the atmosphere with fiery explosions. He vanished into another portal and appeared back on the surface of the planet.

Outside of his home, Armond stood with Abby and Dan. Their gaze was averted to the sky as Hayden approached them. Their faces were all struck with horror-filled awe as they watched enormous fireballs tear across the heavens.

"Do something!" Dan urged Hayden.

"Take cover," Hayden replied.

The sounds of impact could already be heard in the distance. Hayden focused his energy. A blinding point of light radiated from Hayden's chest. The amulet pulsed so fiercely that the waves of energy it produced were audible. A forcefield encircled Hayden, and the light from his chest joined with it as it grew.

Abby, Dan, and Armond were forced to close their eyes and cover their heads as the light grew in intensity. Even then, the light still seeped in as if it were permeating their flesh and bone.

"It hurts!" Abby screamed in pain as she and the others burrowed themselves underneath Armond's car in an attempt to escape the light.

Hayden launched his hands out to his sides. With a tremor-inducing shockwave, the energy-saturated forcefield pulsed outward from his body and into the atmosphere.

With the pain now subsided, the others crawled from their hiding spot and opened their eyes. The entire group watched together as Hayden's burst of energy vaporized all of the remaining pieces of Ceres still in the air.

"What did that?" Abby asked, her voice shaking and

tears running down her cheeks.

"Kali," Hayden replied. "She did that. She fought me, and then when I kept her from taking the amulet, she blew up an entire tiny planet and sent it through a portal toward Earth."

"Unbelievable," Armond muttered.

"I know you guys all heard that, too," Dan said. "Some of those actually hit the ground."

"He's right," Armond admitted. "You should all check on family and friends to ensure they're okay."

"True," Hayden added. "I'm going to have to just fly to each place to check on people. It turns out that Kali can apparently track my portals. That's how she knew to show up at Abby's place right after I got there."

"Okay, we'll all meet back here in a few hours?" Dan confirmed.

The group all shook their heads in agreement. Abby and Dan took off in his car while Armond walked into his house to call his brother. Hayden sighed as he prepared himself for the worst. Rising slowly into the air at first, Hayden renewed his resolve and streaked across the sky toward Nevada to check on his parents first.

ضوء النهار

Chapter Five

Daylight

Hayden gathered his thoughts and took another mental tally of everyone he had checked on so far. He was almost sure that he had accounted for all his family members and most of his friends. Some of them were a little beat up, but luckily, no one had any critical injuries. Again, he ran through the list in his head. He was frantic, shaken, and hadn't had anything to drink in hours. He couldn't shake the feeling that he wasn't done yet.

The television newscast droned on in the background of the room, "...and several cities in the Los Angeles area have suffered damage, mostly minor. However, there are some notable exceptions of major damage in the cities of Santa Clarita, Fillmore, Oxnard, and Camarillo."

Hayden's mind subconsciously caught the final words

of the news anchor. Camarillo. The Hensley's lived there. He ran out the door and took flight toward the city.

"How could I fucking forget Camarillo?" Hayden lambasted himself in his thoughts.

As he approached the town, he was shocked to see the extent of the devastation sprawled out in front of him. Craters pocked the ground for miles, and fires raged in the heart of the city, smoke billowing into the sky as firefighters struggled to attack the widespread carnage.

Hayden touched down on the street of his family's friends, Gabe and Martha Hensley. As he ran in the direction of the home, he quickly realized that the house he was familiar with seeing in the past was no more. The structure was partially collapsed in spots and smoldering in other areas.

Hayden walked through the obliterated front door and examined the scene. Furniture and various belongings were scattered everywhere. He walked toward the living room to find the roof caved in near the far wall. As he scanned the area, he quickly found the first victim of the day that he knew personally. Gabe's nineteen-year-old son, Pete, lay near the couch in a pool of blood. Hayden walked over to check his pulse, which confirmed his fear.

A faint noise from the rear of the residence

attracted Hayden's attention. He made his way down the hall, stepping over broken picture frames, pieces of shattered rafter beams, and other debris. As he opened the door of the master bedroom, he saw Gabe on his knees next to the bed. Gabe was holding his wife's hand. Her body had been partially crushed by a large piece of the roof that had caved in while they were in bed watching the morning news. Gabe was sobbing at the sudden catastrophic loss. As Hayden approached Gabe, he noticed that he had several large pieces of a splintered wood beam protruding from his back. The wounds were steadily bleeding.

Gabe turned around slowly as he heard Hayden walking toward him through the shattered glass and debris on the floor of the bedroom.

"Hayden?" Gabe questioned as he realized who was there.

"Yeah, it's me, Gabe," Hayden replied, not quite knowing what to say in the moment.

"She's gone…" Gabe muttered and paused. "Did you… happen to see my kids? I can't even get up. It hurts too much."

"I ummm… I saw Pete in the living room," Hayden reluctantly replied. "I'm sorry, Gabe, he didn't make it."

Gabe sniffled as he unsuccessfully tried to hold back more tears. "Oh my God," he managed. "What about…"

His question was interrupted by the sound of footsteps crunching through the trail of glass in the bedroom doorway.

"What… happened?" the girl said shakily, clearly in a confused daze.

"Elle!" Gabe called out with labored breathing. "Are you okay?"

"I think so…" she replied. After a couple moments, she finally recognized the severity of the scene and stumbled over to Gabe. She began to cry as she noticed her deceased mother and badly injured father.

Hayden noted that Elle appeared to be mostly uninjured as she passed him. She had some cuts and abrasions scattered all over her limbs… she was clearly in a state of shock… but she had no visible wounds, no large spots of blood on her clothing, and nothing appeared to be broken in terms of bones.

"Dad, are you okay?" Elle asked Gabe, fearing that she already knew the answer.

"Elle, listen to me," Gabe responded. "I need you to be strong. You need to get out of here. I need you to go with Hayden."

Elle looked at Hayden and then back to Gabe. Not wanting to let go so easily, Elle replied. "But… Dad we can get you some help. We can..." Her voice trailed off as despair continued to set in.

Gabe motioned for Hayden to come closer. Hayden knelt down next to him and then placed his hand on Gabe's shoulder.

"Hayden, you need to take her and keep her safe," Gabe begged, his breath labored and his voice now gurgling as blood dripped from his lips. "Do this for me and Martha. In a couple minutes, she won't have any family left. My parents and my in-laws are dead. My wife and I were only children… Please promise me."

Hayden looked over at Elle, her eyes now steadily shedding tears. "I promise," he solemnly replied.

As Hayden began to turn his gaze back toward Gabe, he felt the tension in his shoulder loosen. It was as if Hayden's promise was the last thing that Gabe needed before passing on. He drew his last breath immediately after. Hayden hung his head in remorse for a moment at the passing of a friend. He and Elle then looked at each other, unable to process the entirety of the tragic events that had just unfolded.

The moment was interrupted by the sound of a large explosion in the house next door. Hayden rose to his feet and grabbed Elle's hand. "We need to get out of here," he told her.

The two made their way through the debris and

out the front door of the house. Elle was astonished at the extensive damage in the neighborhood.

"Elle, I'm going to get us out of here. This might be a little weird, but I'm just going to need you to trust me… okay?" Hayden told her, not sure if she had any knowledge of his powers. Though the news had briefly run stories on the Alva'ci and the agents of fate, the government quickly stepped in and shut down any mention of the events.

Hayden hadn't seen Gabe or his family in about nine months. The last time had been when Hayden's mother and father were visiting the Hensley's for a couple weeks. He had always had a friendly relationship with Elle and her brother Pete. However, he hadn't seen Elle since her fifteenth birthday, which she celebrated during that last visit.

"Okay," Elle replied. "I trust you."

Another explosion from a nearby home rattled the ground beneath them. Fiery debris rained down on the surrounding houses. Hayden put his arm around Elle and instructed her to hold on. She looked confused but put both her arms around Hayden as if she were hugging him.

"Yeah, she definitely doesn't know about these powers yet," Hayden thought to himself after seeing the confused look on her face.

Hayden tightened his hold on Elle and gently lifted a

few feet off the ground. Elle's eyes widened, and she screamed in panic. She momentarily loosened her grip on Hayden in fear. Once she realized that action might result in her falling, Elle immediately returned to clinging onto Hayden for dear life.

"It's okay. You're okay Elle," Hayden told her, trying to be reassuring. "I've got you. Like I said, this might be weird, but I'll explain the whole flying thing once we're out of here. A lot has happened recently."

Elle seemed to relax a little with Hayden's words. She loosened from a death-grip bear hug to a very firm grasp. Hayden rose off the ground gradually another several feet.

"You okay?" he asked her.

"Yeah, just please don't drop me," she replied.

"Elle, I would never drop you."

As she nodded in acknowledgment, Hayden took off further into the sky. He kept his ascent to a slow but steady pace. After a few minutes, Hayden touched down on the shores of Paradise Cove beach in Malibu. The beach was empty. Hayden asked Elle to stay on the shore while he went into the nearby cafe to grab them something to drink.

Hayden walked inside and found the cafe utterly devoid of activity. He grabbed two bottles of water from a beverage cooler and made his way back outside. As he walked back toward the beach, his mind wandered to the destructive events of the morning... then to Kali and what she had become.

As he continued, Hayden snapped back into the present. He looked out to the shoreline and saw Elle. She had removed her shoes and let her feet soak in the waves as they lapped up onto the beach. Her blonde hair, disheveled from both the events of the morning and their recent flight, gently blew in the breeze. As Hayden approached her, Elle looked over at him. She managed a faint smile, though her mind was still reeling from tragedy.

The moment took Hayden by surprise. Not the smile... but the sudden feeling that took over his body. The sense of deja vu hit him like a ton of bricks. In an instant, he realized...

"Holy shit," Hayden said to himself. "This was all in my dream. This is the Abassilon Prophecy."

He looked into Elle's eyes, now seemingly a little more hopeful than just a half hour ago. She reached out her hand for Hayden.

"Take off your shoes," she suggested.

Hayden kicked off his shoes and socks and took her hand. Elle pulled him up next to her as the wave came in and covered their feet. He smiled back at her... but in the back of his mind, he feared for his ability to keep her safe in the coming days. The feeling was strange to him. It was the first time he had felt fear in recent memory.

Hayden pushed the thoughts away and attempted to simply enjoy the moment of peace during an otherwise tragic day. After several minutes of silently standing in the ocean together, Hayden and Elle grabbed their shoes and walked back toward the cafe building.

"What now?" asked Elle.

"Now we get back down to Orange County. We can come up with some sort of plan with my group... and you can get cleaned up and get some rest. Are you ready?"

Elle put her arms around Hayden again, and they took flight. They headed southeast toward Fullerton, this time at a faster pace. A few minutes later, they touched down outside Hayden's apartment and found Dan and Armond outside talking.

"Hey guys, anything new?" Hayden asked as they walked up.

"Uhhh, I mean, apparently so," Dan replied inquisitively, obviously in reference to Elle. "Who's the girl?"

"This is Elle," Hayden replied and then addressed her. "Elle, this is my best friend, Dan, and my... new friend, Armond."

"Good to meet you, Elle," Dan greeted her, then

directed his conversation back to Hayden. "But, like, who is she?"

"Long story…" Hayden started, "I went to check on her family up in Camarillo…"

"Oh shit," Dan interrupted, knowing what the news had been saying about the destruction in the city. "I'm so sorry… Is she…"

"Yeah," Hayden replied, knowing that Dan was really asking if she was all that was left of her family.

Dan walked over and gave Elle a hug.

"Well, Elle, you couldn't be anywhere safer than here with Hayden," Dan offered what he hoped was a calming reassurance.

"I know, thank you," Elle replied.

Armond interjected, "Hayden, we need to do something about Kali."

"Yeah, I know," Hayden agreed. "Give me a few minutes, Armond. I'm going to take Elle inside and let her get cleaned up."

Armond nodded in acknowledgment as he realized he had abruptly changed the tone of the conversation. Hayden patted him on the shoulder as he walked past and took Elle into the apartment.

"We'll figure everything out later, but for now, here's

the bathroom. You can take a shower, and then if you need to rest, my room is right over there," Hayden told her, pointing down the hallway to his bedroom door.

"Thanks," Elle replied as she walked into the bathroom and looked around. Hayden took a towel from the hallway closet and placed it on the bathroom counter.

"Oh, damn," he said in a sudden realization of her dirty and tattered clothes. "You've got nothing to wear or anything…"

Hayden wandered down the hallway and then reappeared a moment later with a pen and a notepad.

"Here, write down the sizes you wear, and I'll go get you some clothes while you shower," Hayden told Elle.

"You don't have to… are you sure?" she replied, not wanting to be a nuisance. "I can just wear these again."

"No, you can't… those are all torn up," Hayden insisted. "It's not a problem at all, Elle."

She smiled, took the pen and notepad from Hayden's hand, quickly jotted down a few lines, and handed the list back to him.

"Alright, I got ya. Be back in a couple minutes." Hayden said as he walked out of the bathroom and closed the door behind him. Elle fired up the shower and tossed her clothes in the corner.

Hayden walked outside to meet Armond and Dan again.

"Are we ready?" Armond asked.

"Negative," Hayden replied. "Gotta run a quick errand, and then I'm all yours."

"Errand?" Armond inquired, slightly annoyed that something was again coming before a much-needed strategy session.

Hayden saw the look of exasperation on Armond's face. "Yeah, one quick errand, Armond… then we'll get to what we need to do."

Hayden didn't give him a chance to respond, immediately taking flight and heading northward. In a few moments, he touched down in the parking lot of Target. As Hayden walked up to the entrance of the store, he looked down and examined the piece of paper in his hand:

Shirt - Small

Bra - 32A

Pants - 1

Underwear - Small

"Okay, this should be fairly simple… hopefully." Hayden thought to himself.

As he entered the store, Hayden observed how busy the place was and remembered why he always hated shopping in the middle of the day. He was in a hurry. After a moment of consideration, Hayden grasped the amulet in his right hand. He pushed a thought into the mind of every person in the store that effectively froze them in place. He then walked up to a cash register and touched the casing of the security camera on the pole above it. He focused his mind and sent a surge of electricity through the camera's circuitry. Somewhere in a hidden electrical room, the camera system's power supply overloaded, and the video recorders malfunctioned. There would be no trace of Hayden in the store today.

"I just saved the world. A little light shoplifting isn't going to hurt anyone," Hayden said to himself. "I'll just spend some extra next time I come back."

Hayden made his way past the stationary people in the aisles and over to the juniors department. He examined the list one more time and made his way through the racks.

"Let's see… I should probably at least try to find some stuff that isn't horrendous looking," Hayden mused as he sifted through the selection of shirts, now slightly feeling like he had volunteered himself for an impromptu test of sorts. He didn't want to take so long that Elle would be done with her shower and waiting around for him to return, but he also didn't want to show up and have her eternally question his sense of fashion. He finally selected a couple shirts and made sure they were the correct size.

"Okay, pretty easy so far," Hayden mumbled to himself.

Arriving in the pants section, he made better time in identifying some adequately stylish jeans. He grabbed a pair. As he walked through the sleepwear aisles, he grabbed a pair of light flannel pajama shorts and a comfortable-looking cami top. Upon arriving in intimates, Hayden picked out a bra and placed a pack of panties under his arm.

"One last thing," he said to himself as he grabbed a pack of socks from a nearby rack.

Hayden started making his way to the front of the store. As he passed by aisle endcaps, he added a toothbrush and a bundle of hair ties just in case.

"Okay, we should be good…" he thought. "I should have anything she might need until I take her shopping later tonight."

Hayden arrived at a cash register and grabbed a couple plastic bags from behind the counter. After placing all of the items in the bags, he walked out the exit door. He stopped for a moment once he was outside, as if he had just remembered something. Hayden grasped the amulet again and pushed another thought to all the occupants of the building, releasing them from their involuntary standstill. Now satisfied with the outcome of his trip, Hayden took off in flight toward his apartment.

As Hayden landed outside his apartment, Dan and Armond sat and watched as he walked past them without a word. Hayden walked in and arrived at the bathroom door. The shower was still running.

"I made pretty good time," he proudly said to himself.

Hayden cracked the bathroom door open and placed the bags on the counter.

"Hey, Elle, all your new stuff is on the counter."

Elle cracked open the frosted glass shower door and peeked her head out, observing the shopping bags.

"Thank you!" she exclaimed.

"You're welcome," Hayden replied. "If you need anything else, just let me know. I'll be outside with Dan and Armond."

Hayden closed the bathroom door, and Elle resumed her shower. Dan and Armond stared at Hayden as he walked back out the front door.

"No more errands?" Dan asked jokingly.

"We're all good for now," Hayden replied. "So, what's

the plan?"

"Well, we don't know where Kali is…" Armond said. "Can you sense her location at all?"

"No, not really. Only when she's really close by," Hayden replied.

"So we are most likely going to have to wait until she decides to reappear, unfortunately," Armond continued. "That's not ideal for us, but we don't really have a choice. Right now, Hayden, you should focus on using that amulet of yours to hone your powers more and maybe see if it can enable you to track Kali. I wouldn't be that surprised if all that energy from the Alva'ci strengthened the amulet."

"Yeah, the power inside of it has definitely been amplified," Hayden concurred. "I haven't had much time yet to really experiment with it, but I will get to it."

"Dan, can you go to the others and ask them to prepare for a meeting if we find Kali?" Armond asked.

"Sure thing!" Dan agreed.

"Perfect. I'm going to go study the texts and prophecies to see if there's anything I missed before that can help us," Armond added.

"Oh, that reminds me…" Hayden interjected. "The Abassilon Prophecy. I felt it when Elle and I stopped for a break in Malibu."

"Hmm… that is intriguing." Armond mused aloud. "The dream must have been a precursor for the event. As we discussed before, Abassilon has never been considered to have that much consequence in the grand scheme of things. It probably just means that this girl, Elle, may play some sort of important role in your life. Let's just hope it's not a tragic role."

"Oh, that doesn't sound ominous or depressing at all," Dan said mockingly as he walked off toward his car. "See you guys soon!"

"I'll be in touch, Hayden. Let me know if you figure anything out about the amulet," Armond said before heading to his own vehicle.

Hayden waved as he opened the front door to his apartment, and then he proceeded inside. He found Elle in the front room, sitting on the couch and eating some Pop-Tarts.

"I was hungry," she told Hayden.

"Of course," he replied. "Anything you need is yours, Elle. How did everything fit?"

"Everything fits perfectly. Thank you."

"Give me a little bit to relax, and then we can head back to the store and do some actual shopping for you. I just grabbed the bare necessities, but we'll get you everything you need."

"Hayden, you don't have to…" she replied.

"Elle, don't act like you're a burden to me…" Hayden answered. "I want you to be happy and know that you'll be well taken care of. I want to do that."

Elle replied with a smile. Though the pain of the morning's events weighed heavily on her, she tried to appear strong and act normal.

"So, what's up with the flying thing?" she asked after a few moments.

"Oh, yeah, that…" Hayden replied. "I guess a lot has changed since we last saw each other. The flying is actually just me manipulating air with my powers."

"Powers?" Elle asked, still confused.

"That's right, you don't know about the powers," Hayden remembered. "It's probably going to be easier for me to just show you."

Hayden led Elle to the back patio of the apartment. Once they were outside, Hayden continued. "Do you remember hearing anything about the 'end of the world' thing a few months ago? Right around that time, I developed several powers. I was there helping fight off the alien creature."

Hayden raised both his palms toward the sky. The symbols of darkness and electricity appeared on each of his hands, and the effects shot upwards into a nearby cloud. The cloud grew dark and immediately began to pour rain over the patio. Lightning erupted across the sky. Elle looked up at the cloud and then over at Hayden in astonishment. The thunder rattled the windows of the apartment. Hayden activated the power of air and promptly scattered the cloud into tiny specks across the sky.

"Wow," Elle said, practically speechless. "You've definitely changed a lot."

Hayden laughed. "Yeah, I guess so."

"What's the necklace you're wearing?"

"The amulet…" Hayden replied. "This used to be a shard of rock that I was stabbed with. It's made of the same material as the creature that tried to end the world. I changed the stone's shape into this form. It sort of amplifies my powers, you could say."

"What else can you do?" Elle asked.

"I can cook pretty good," Hayden said jokingly. "Uhh, but for real, I can control fire, air, water, electricity, light, darkness, nature, energy… and the mind to some extent. I'm still learning new things, honestly."

"So, like everything," Elle replied. "You can pretty much do anything."

"Ummm, yeah," Hayden answered.

"That's pretty amazing. You'll have to show me some

more… maybe without the thunder next time," she said.

"Of course. What do you say we relax for a bit first?" Hayden replied while stepping back into the living room.

"That would be… perfect. I'm so tired," Elle said while yawning.

Hayden smiled and sunk back into the couch cushion, flicking on the television. Within a minute, Hayden had dozed off. Elle ate the last piece of her now cold Pop-Tart, rested her head on Hayden's shoulder, and fell asleep.

Three hours later, Hayden woke up to the distinct sound of SpongeBob SquarePants laughing on the television. He opened his eyes and found Elle, still fast asleep, collapsed against him. Hayden moved slightly, cradling her head in his hand. Elle didn't wake up.

"She wasn't kidding about being tired." Hayden thought to himself. "I guess I can use the time to experiment with the amulet like Armond wanted."

Hayden picked Elle up and carried her into the bedroom. He placed her on the bed and pulled the comforter up over her. She momentarily awoke.

"Hey, get some more rest," he said softly.

Elle smiled and then closed her eyes again, quickly falling back asleep.

Hayden ventured out of the bedroom and onto the

back patio. He clutched the amulet in his hand and closed his eyes, focusing on each of the powers one at a time. He felt an intense well of increased power within the amulet. He began searching for more, looking for new ways to manipulate his abilities.

Hayden honed in on his Energy and Ane'illuminus powers. What he discovered was something he knew Armond would want to hear about. He opened his eyes again and found that the afternoon had become night. He looked at his watch, 8:30 p.m. He had spent seven hours on the back patio in what seemed like minutes.

Hayden got up and walked back inside, wandering to the kitchen. He chugged an entire glass of water before heading back down the hallway to his bedroom. Elle was still asleep. He gently woke her.

Elle opened her eyes and stared at Hayden. "Hi," she eventually said.

"Hello," Hayden replied with a chuckle. "Quite the nap."

"I feel so much better… is it still today?" Elle asked.

"Yep. Well, I mean, it's tonight now," Hayden replied. "We should probably do that shopping pretty quickly here before the stores close."

Elle sprung up. "Oh, you're right. I forgot about that.

Let me just brush my teeth again real quick, and I'll be ready to go."

Hayden figured that was probably an excellent idea for him also after sitting on the patio in a trance for the last several hours.

"Okay, I'll meet you out in the living room," Hayden replied.

After a few minutes, Elle and Hayden convened in the living room and then made their way outside.

"So, car or air travel?" Hayden asked her jokingly.

"Let's be normal and take the car this time," Elle said as she laughed.

They got in the car and returned to Target, where they picked up a few more pairs of clothes, makeup, and other essentials. Hayden made sure to pay for his purchases this time around.

Hayden drove over to Brea Mall, and they made procurements at several more stores, including a new phone for Elle. After filling the car's back seat with shopping bags, Hayden noticed that he was insanely hungry.

"So first of all, good call on using the car… I don't think I would even be able to get off the ground with all those bags," Hayden joked. "Also, are you as hungry as I am?"

"I am soooo hungry," Elle replied. "Those Pop-Tarts

did not hold me over."

Hayden drove to In n' Out, and they promptly devoured their meals. Around 10:30 p.m., they arrived back at the apartment and carried all of Elle's new things inside.

"Thank you again, Hayden," Elle said.

"You're welcome," he replied. "So, as far as sleeping, the couch pulls out into a bed. I can sleep on that until I get the guest bedroom ready. Unfortunately, I let Dan have the bed that was in there when his broke last week."

"No, I'll sleep on the pullout," Elle insisted. "You can sleep in your bed."

"Okay… I mean, it's not a problem either way," Hayden replied.

"Take your bed, Hayden," Elle again insisted. "You've already done so much for me today… I mean, you like literally saved my life."

"Alright," Hayden relented and pulled out the sofa bed, preparing it for Elle with a blanket and some pillows from the hall closet. "I'm off to bed then. Sleep well."

"You too," Elle responded.

Hayden went to his bedroom and changed into his pajamas, once again falling asleep within minutes of closing his eyes.

Elle changed into the pajama shorts and cami top that

Hayden had gotten her earlier in the day and then lay on the pullout bed in the front room. She stared at the ceiling for about half an hour, pondering all of the events from that day. She felt a broad spectrum of emotions, from grief to happiness, as she focused on everything that had happened.

Eventually, she got up and headed to the bathroom... the large soda at dinner had finally caught up with her. As she exited the bathroom, Elle stood in the doorway and found herself looking down the hallway. After a few moments, she walked over to Hayden's bedroom door and opened it. Hayden was fast asleep. Elle stood there for a few minutes, looking over at him.

Elle walked closer to the foot of the bed and stood in place for a few more minutes, again contemplating the day. She knew that if the morning had played out differently... if Hayden hadn't shown up to check on her family, she would probably be dead. The thought scared her. Simultaneously, she felt comfort in the fact that she was saved but also guilt that she was the only member of her family to make it out alive.

Elle moved from the foot of the bed and walked over to the side of it. She pulled back the comforter slightly and sat down on the mattress, momentarily questioning herself in her mind... she laid down and slid under the comforter, moving closer to Hayden. He was still asleep. Elle rested her head on his chest and placed her arm over him. Now… she fell right to sleep.

❛ ❛ ❛ ❛ ❛ ❛

The next morning, Hayden awoke, startled to find Elle in bed with him. He recounted the previous night in his head and determined that she definitely wasn't in the room when he had fallen asleep. Hayden placed his hand on her arm and tried to wake her. After a few moments, Elle opened her eyes and smiled at Hayden.

"Good morning," she said sleepily.

"Hey there… good morning," Hayden replied. "Little ways from the sofa bed, eh?"

Elle realized Hayden must be wondering why she was beside him when he fell asleep alone.

"Ohh…" she hesitated. "Is this okay? I had so many thoughts running through my head last night that I couldn't sleep. I guess I was a bit scared after everything that happened. I just felt safer being in here with you…"

Before Hayden could come up with an answer, the amulet began to vibrate furiously and glow on the nightstand next to the bed. Hayden sat up and grabbed it.

"What's happening?" Elle asked, concerned.

"I don't know," Hayden replied.

The sliver of daylight coming in through the curtains disappeared suddenly. Hayden sprung up out of bed and ran down the hallway toward the front door, with Elle following right behind him. As he opened the front door and the two of them stepped outside, Hayden noted the darkness. A figure appeared in the sky, the only faint source of light. It was Kali. She disappeared instantly, and the sunlight returned to the sky.

"What was that?" Elle asked, with fear evident in the tone of her voice.

"Nothing good," Hayden replied.

Hayden's cell phone rang from the bedroom. They ran back down the hall... it was Armond calling. Hayden picked up the phone.

"Did you see that?" Armond asked right away.

"Yeah, she was right there for a minute and then gone," Hayden replied.

ဆ ဆ ဆ ဆ ဆ ဆ

"We must confront the fact that Kali may be so far gone that we cannot save her. The corruption seems to have completely taken over her mind," Armond told the group.

"I can't believe that she actually sent all those meteorites down to crash into the planet," Abby said. "How many people died because of her lust for power?"

The group sat in Hayden's front room and discussed the aftermath of the recent disaster and their next steps. During the meeting, Hayden repeatedly zoned in and out of his own thoughts, but tried to maintain his focus and pay attention to the words of his friends. Elle sat on the couch next to Hayden, remaining silent, but soaking up all of the information.

"Even if she goes back to normal," Dan added. "What she did is going to land her in prison for the rest of her life. I hate to say it, but Kali probably isn't going to have a happy ending here."

"What do you think, Hayden?" Abby asked.

Hayden stood from the couch and paused for a moment in the center of the room, apparently lost in thought. Elle gazed at him and then exchanged glances with Dan and Abby as if she were asking them if he was okay. There were no answers to be found in the group's collective confusion. Hayden looked toward the ceiling and released a sigh before heading toward the front door, detouring only slightly to grab his wireless earbuds for his phone.

Elle, Dan, and Abby watched from the open door as Hayden made his way to the front lawn. Everyone stood silently at the threshold, waiting for something to happen, when they noticed a distinct drop in the temperature. Hayden put his earphones in and fiddled with his phone to play a song.

The slight breeze came to a standstill. The sky began to fill with ominous-looking clouds, blocking out the sun. The previously bright and peaceful day became foreboding.

"I think he's having an emo moment," Dan half-joked to the others.

Abby shot Dan a look to show her disdain for the joke, although admittedly, she partly agreed with his assessment. Elle's hands clung to the door frame as she continued to watch with growing consternation.

The back of Hayden's hands both lit up with symbols as the blanket of clouds turned the sky black. Lightning crackled fiercely as it cut from one edge of the sky to the other. For a moment afterward, the air was perfectly still. Hayden looked up as he raised his arms to his sides. The stillness was pierced by a sudden torrential downpour of rain.

"Should we do something?" Elle asked the others.

Abby looked over at her and could see that she was worried. "I think he just needs a moment. The impromptu storm is a little dramatic, but I don't think you need to worry too much."

The rain soaked Hayden's clothes as he stood frozen in place on the lawn. Droplets pelted his face and outstretched arms. As he moved his left hand up toward the sky, the amulet began to glow, and a forcefield flickered into place around him. Elle, Abby, and Dan exchanged confused looks until their attention was drawn back by a bolt of lightning that poured down onto the forcefield.

"Damn…" Dan mumbled in amazement. Elle and Abby stood silently with their mouths agape in shock.

As Hayden dropped his arms back down to his sides, the lightning and rain stopped as abruptly as they had begun. The clouds dissipated, returning the afternoon sun to complete the task of drying the landscape. Hayden removed his earphones and walked back toward the apartment.

"You good, buddy?" Dan asked as Hayden approached.

Hayden nodded, and the group filtered back inside. Elle hung back near Hayden while Abby and Dan returned to the front room.

"Are you okay? Do you want to talk about what just happened… or anything?" Elle asked in a hushed voice.

"I'm okay. I'm just finally processing some things that I've come to accept. It's been a long time coming."

Hayden walked into the kitchen and grabbed a couple of sodas from the fridge. He handed one to Elle and took a sip out of the other.

"I'll talk to you about it," Hayden continued. "But tonight, let's all just go out and grab some dinner and lighten up the mood a little bit. You and I can talk tomorrow when we don't have any company."

Elle smiled and nodded her head in agreement. She felt a distinct sense of nostalgia when Hayden agreed to talk to her. She was happy that he wasn't closing himself off with whatever was bothering him.

"I'm going to change out of these wet clothes, and then we can take off for dinner," Hayden told Elle.

"Okay, I'm ready to go," she replied.

Hayden began to walk down the hallway. His waterlogged shoes audibly marked each step he took until he disappeared into the bedroom.

"Oh, can you grab my purse from the room?" Elle called out in a raised voice down the hallway before joining Abby and Dan in the front room.

Hayden reappeared five minutes later with a fresh set of dry clothes and Elle's purse in hand.

"Let's go eat!" Hayden beckoned.

قدر
Chapter Six

Moira

Elle woke up the next morning to sunlight peeking through the window. The sheer white curtains danced along the cool breeze that was seeping into the room from outside. Atop the long dresser that stood below the window were several bags of clothing, decor, and other items that she and Hayden had not put away the night before.

As she slowly rose from her new bed, Elle heard faint sounds coming from the kitchen. Now that her mind and body were transitioning from tranquil slumber to waking alertness, Elle noticed a distinctly familiar aroma. Wisps of cinnamon and vanilla snuck under the door and filled the room. They fought against the earthy and floral notes floating through the window on the breeze. She wandered from her bedroom to the dining room to find Hayden already preparing breakfast. Elle sat at the kitchen table and shook her head at Hayden once he looked over to see her.

"Is your plan to just spoil me forever?" she asked him.

"Am I?" Hayden answered with a question.

"I can clearly smell that you're making my favorite thing for breakfast," she replied.

"Oh, you thought this was for you?" Hayden teased.

Elle stood and walked over to the kitchen, where Hayden was placing slices of French toast on a plate. She stopped right beside him and placed her hands on her hips.

"It better be for me!" she playfully fought back. "I know that you know I love your French toast recipe."

"Of course, that's why I made it," Hayden relented in his teasing as he handed Elle a plate loaded with several slices slathered with butter and drenched in syrup. Elle gleefully carried it back to the table and sat down.

"Like I said, you're spoiling me," Elle said as she took her first bite. The look on her face unmistakably relayed the satisfaction of her taste buds. "Not that I'm complaining at all."

"I'm not spoiling you," Hayden replied. "I just know certain things that you like, and I'm doing them for you."

"Isn't that the definition of the phrase?" Elle asked while laughing. "But totally honest, I really do appreciate everything that you've done for me. Thank you."

"You're welcome. Like I said before, I'm going to take care of you. Whatever you need, don't even hesitate to ask," Hayden told her as he sat at the table and started eating his breakfast.

While Hayden cleaned up the mess from cooking, Elle took a shower. They were going to head out to a few more stores to gather more items. Once Hayden saw that Elle had returned to her room to finish getting ready, he jumped in the shower.

Hayden walked out to the front yard to find Elle sitting in the grass, enjoying the mild sun and cool morning breeze. He sat down next to her and took in the calmness of the day.

"So, are you still going to talk to me about what happened yesterday?" Elle reminded him.

"Yeah, of course," Hayden answered. "I'm sure you're probably aware that Kali and I were together. We had dated shortly a few years ago, and then she moved away. She came back to town when her sister died last year, and we rekindled things. It was going pretty good, and then the world decided that it wanted to try and end. Myself and a couple others fought off the alien creature, but at the last moment it kidnapped Kali. After seven months of preparing, I finally rescued her. But she made a huge mistake and dabbled with the creature's power. It corrupted her mind. I asked her to let me help her. In response, she attacked me and then sent all those meteorites flying into the planet."

Hayden took a deep breath and thought for a moment.

"I bet that's taken a toll on you," Elle said compassionately.

"It did," Hayden agreed. "But what you saw yesterday… that was me finally accepting things for what they are. I saw first-hand that Kali is too far gone for me to help. What she has done is pretty much unforgivable. That was me letting go."

"Thank you for trusting me enough to tell me," Elle said. "If you need to talk about anything…"

The last word that Elle said echoed in Hayden's ears as a haunting crackle of lightning stung their ears. They jumped to their feet in panic from the sudden freak occurrence. As they looked to the sky, Kali appeared, floating twenty feet above them.

"Let's end this!" Kali called out to Hayden.

Instinctively, Elle clung to Hayden in fear at the ominous threat. Kali waved her hand in front of herself. Hayden had barely noticed the portal appear beneath his feet before he and Elle fell into it.

❧ ❧ ❧ ❧ ❧ ❧

Hayden and Elle landed with an audible thud on the surface of a foreign planet. The ground was covered in a grey-colored sand. The landscape was barren of any water, flora, and fauna. Instead of the familiar warm glow of the sun, they looked up to see the spectacularly eerie light from the accretion disk of a supermassive black hole. Hayden looked over at Elle to make sure that she was okay. It appeared that the effects of his powers on the surrounding area were indeed allowing her to breathe and remain warm also.

"Where are we?" Elle asked as they stood up.

Kali appeared from another nearby portal.

"Welcome to planet XRGTC-2020, or, as I like to call it, Moira," Kali said as she touched down on the surface. "Fun fact: that black hole you see came from a star that went supernova when I was five years old."

"Let me guess," Hayden replied. "This is allegedly where I will die? Moira is Greek for fate."

"You always were really smart, Hayden," Kali responded. "I see that I unintentionally sucked your little friend here into the portal also. That sucks for her. Once you're dead, she won't enjoy the protection of your powers. Her death will be much more slow and painful than yours."

"You're not going to win this, Kali," Hayden retorted. "And I won't let that happen to her either."

"Oh, you'd rather she die quickly?" Kali mockingly asked. "I can oblige that."

Kali quickly fired off a blast of energy at Elle. Hayden reacted and brought a Chantiatus forcefield up around her, deflecting the attack. Kali laughed at Hayden's predicament. He would not only have to fight her but protect Elle as well.

"Who is this girl anyway?" Kali inquired, obviously annoyed.

"It's Elle. Remember, my family hung out with hers growing up," Hayden replied. "Your insane attack on Earth killed her family."

"Oh, that's too bad," Kali said, her tone obviously cold and uncaring.

Elle's demeanor changed with Kali's callous and malevolent attitude toward the irreparable damage she had done to Elle's family.

"Are you going to cry?" Kali mocked her.

Hayden had heard enough. He sent a blast of energy hurtling toward Kali. The reaction caught her by surprise and sent her flying back twenty feet into the dust.

"A little bit protective are we?" Kali taunted as she stood and brushed the dust off her clothes. "Was it something I said?"

Hayden attacked again, but this time, Kali was prepared and deflected the incoming blast. She immediately retaliated with an attack of her own. The ensuing back-and-forth volley of gradually strengthening energy blasts seemed to end in another stalemate between the two.

"Why delay the inevitable, Hayden?" Kali taunted once again.

Before Hayden could respond, Kali focused a continuous blast of energy from her left hand onto Elle's forcefield. Hayden fired off an attack at Kali, but she deftly redirected it with her other hand. As Elle's forcefield began to flicker and weaken with the prolonged barrage against it, Hayden stepped in front of her, sending the blast of energy scattering in all directions. Elle cowered on her hands and knees, attempting to hide herself from Kali's onslaught.

Kali seized the opportunity to act. With Hayden focused on protecting Elle, he was temporarily distracted. Kali raised her right hand again and pulled a small stone up from the surface of the planet from behind Hayden. With a flick of her wrist, the rock accelerated toward Hayden like a bullet and pierced his flesh. Entering his lower back, the rock flew clean through and exited his abdomen. The shock and reeling pain immediately caused Hayden to collapse onto the ground. Kali ended her initial diversion of an attack.

Elle knelt down at Hayden's side and put pressure on the exit wound in an attempt to curb the bleeding. Kali walked toward the duo with the confident stride of victory.

"Looks like I can predict the future," she taunted as she continued to close the gap between them.

In his panic, Hayden devised a plan that he hoped would at least delay the worst. His hands lit up with symbols of power. Elle covered her eyes with her one free hand to shield them from the blinding light that began to emanate from Hayden.

"Prophesch'naya Con'di Ashante," Hayden chanted, and cast a spell to confuse Kali.

"A little challenge won't stop me," Kali said as she continued on through the intense white light.

Hayden concentrated and pushed a thought into Kali's mind, further disorienting her. She began to stumble around the planet's surface aimlessly.

"This is your plan?" she screamed at Hayden. "This game will only delay the inevitable. I'll simply come back tomorrow and take the amulet from your dead body."

Kali vanished in a flash of orange into a portal. Once

she was gone, Hayden let off the use of his powers and immediately convulsed in pain.

"What can I do?" Elle asked frantically, with tears now running down her face.

"How bad is it bleeding?" Hayden asked through deep breaths.

Elle moved her blood-covered hand and looked at the wound. "Steadily, but not like gushing."

"Okay. We need to get off this planet before she returns," Hayden said. "I'm going to use one of my powers to do a quick check on my body and make sure that rock didn't hit anything important. It's going to look like I'm asleep."

"Alright," Elle replied, but her wavering voice gave away her uncertainty. "Please be careful."

"I will," Hayden told her as he closed his eyes and slipped into the dreamscape.

Thirty minutes later, Hayden awoke. Elle breathed a deep sigh of relief as he opened his eyes. She had continued to hold pressure on Hayden's wound while constantly scanning the area for any threats. Though she had known he was still alive by the presence of his pulse, each passing minute that Hayden was in the dreamscape had intensified her fear of Kali's threats coming true.

"Hey there," Hayden said to her. "Thank you for

taking care of me. How long was I out for? It felt like days to me."

"Only half an hour or so," she replied.

"Okay. Well, I should be fine," Hayden told Elle. "Just need to close up this wound, and we should be able to leave. This is probably going to hurt."

Hayden's left hand lit up with the symbol of Fire, and a small flame lit in his palm. Elle's eyes widened as she realized what his plan was. She grasped onto Hayden's other hand to offer him an outlet for the impending pain. Hayden looked Elle in the eyes as he moved his hand to his abdomen and scorched the wound to cauterize it.

Elle's hand was sore from the resulting grip as Hayden bore through the pain. As he loosened his grip, Hayden sat up.

"Okay, one more time for the back," he told her.

Hayden repeated the process on the entry wound and then let the fire in his hand die out. Elle helped him to his feet.

"Guess I lost a little blood," Hayden said as he looked over to see Elle's hands and parts of her forearms covered in it. "Hold out your hands," he instructed her.

As Elle reached out toward Hayden, he activated the power of Water. He held his hands over hers, and a stream of water descended from them. After Elle scrubbed her hands clean, Hayden redirected the stream toward himself to wash off some of the drying blood on his side.

"You really are full of tricks," Elle joked.

"Yeah, true," Hayden laughed. "Usually, I would have seen that rock coming with one of my powers. I should have seen it coming."

"I feel bad," Elle admitted. "If you weren't distracted by protecting me, you wouldn't have gotten injured."

"No, don't start that," Hayden replied. "It's not your fault at all. I will do whatever I have to in order to protect you. The reason Kali landed a blow is because I let my guard down. I underestimated just how vicious she has become. That's what got me hit."

Elle nodded in silent acceptance. Hayden turned and looked around the vast nothingness of the planet before turning his eyes upward to look at the eerie light in the sky.

"Okay, for my final trick, I'm going to get us out of here," Hayden said, referencing Elle's earlier joke. "Things are going to happen quickly. Obviously, there's no way off this planet other than using a portal, so that's what we're going to do. Since Kali can track my portals, she's going to know we left. So, right when we step out the other side of the portal, I am going to grab you, and we are going to fly, as fast as I can, to some other place. Are you ready?"

"I'm ready," Elle confirmed.

Hayden put his arm around her, opened a portal, and they walked into it.

ભ ભ ભ ભ ભ ભ

Hayden and Elle stepped out of the portal back on Earth. Hayden's plan of immediate flight was delayed by a few seconds when he saw the bleakness of the surroundings. The trees and grass that formerly painted the landscape were burned and withered. The sky was filled with ominous clouds, and thunder rolled endlessly in the distance.

Elle flinched as she felt Hayden grab her and take off in flight. She had also been shocked to see their surroundings and momentarily forgot the plan. Once she regained her composure, Elle tightened her grip around Hayden. He was flying with immense speed. Elle was certain that she wouldn't have been able to breathe were it not for the forcefield Hayden had brought up around them.

After a minute, Hayden touched down in San Diego's Balboa Park. The scene was equally as grim. As Elle and Hayden looked around, they saw no other signs of life. No vehicles lined Park Boulevard, and there were no sounds of traffic from the nearby 163 freeway.

"What is going on?" Elle asked.

"I don't know," Hayden replied. "Let's look around and try to find someone."

As they wandered around, Hayden and Elle came upon the Air and Space Museum. The doors were wide open, though no one was in sight. As they walked inside, they noted the general disarray of the museum. Hayden led Elle over to the front ticket counter. As they peered through the glass, Elle saw something on the wall.

"Hayden, look at that clock," she said with an uneasy voice.

The atomic clock that adorned the wall behind the counter provided a startling revelation. The time was on par with what they had expected, almost one o'clock in the afternoon. However, this particular clock also displayed the current date.

"February 10, 2027?" Elle said, confused by what they were reading. "That can't be right… right?"

Hayden paced around the entryway to the museum for a few moments before letting out a long, distressed sigh. He walked over to a newspaper rack by the front door and saw a stack of flyers. He picked up a flyer and shook the layer of dust off. The headline delivered a simple yet blunt message:

"December 19, 2026 - Evacuate Now!"

"The planet we were on was near a supermassive black hole," Hayden said. "The intense gravitational field must have subjected us to time dilation. We were there for two hours, and apparently, four years have passed here on Earth."

"What?" We're in the future?" Elle exclaimed.

"Well, yeah, it seems that way to us," Hayden answered. "My question is, where is everyone?"

"Can we get back?" Elle asked, her voice now panicky. "That's something you can do, right?"

"Honestly, I don't know," Hayden admitted. "I've taken my fair share of physics courses, but nothing prepares you for this."

Seeking some semblance of normalcy and comfort, Elle embraced Hayden as if she were attempting to hide from the reality of the situation. Hayden returned the embrace and thought about their dilemma.

"I'll get us back, Elle. I promise," Hayden finally told her.

"I trust you," she replied.

Hayden picked up a chair and walked over to a vending machine in the corner of the room. After smashing the glass out, he grabbed a couple of lukewarm water bottles and handed one to Elle.

"First, let's head up to La Jolla," Hayden began communicating his new plan to Elle. "We can swing by UCSD and see if there's anything helpful there. We can always fly up to Goldstone also if we need a radio telescope."

"Okay, I'm ready when you are," Elle said after chugging her bottle of water. "The fact that you already have a plan makes me feel a little better."

After a short flight, Hayden touched down on the campus of UC San Diego. Elle let go of her grip on Hayden and began walking around, looking at all the buildings. Hayden walked over to a campus map and studied it briefly.

"Alright, I think I know where we need to go," Hayden said.

They walked through the abandoned campus until they reached the Revelle College buildings. The atmosphere inside the first building they entered resembled that of the museum from earlier, eerily devoid of human life. However, one improvement they noted was that power was still on across much of the campus.

Settling into a computer lab station, Hayden flicked on the monitor and hoped that it would work. To his surprise, the computer booted up and prompted him for a username and password.

"Well, let's just get around all that," Hayden said with

a chuckle.

Hayden closed his eyes and concentrated while placing his hand on the computer tower. Moments later, the login screen disappeared, and he had access.

"First, I want to see what in the world happened here," he told Elle.

A quick search documented a devastating near-apocalyptic event. Hayden read the story aloud as it roughly detailed an event in December 2026.

"A figure appeared in the sky surrounded by brilliant orange and purple lights. A blinding flash filled the air, and almost instantaneously, reports streamed in of entire metropolitan areas being wiped of human life. Millions of citizens vaporized in seconds. Among the long list of cities to fall victim to the unknown evil force were Los Angeles, New York, Miami, Chicago, Milwaukee, Minneapolis, Seattle, Boston, Baltimore, Vancouver, Mexico City, London, Paris, Moscow, Shanghai, Seoul, Melbourne, and many more. Right away, panic spread throughout the globe. Hours later, another strike occurred. More population centers suffered the same fate. Those cities that had not yet been affected faced mass exile. Areas like Orange County and San Diego saw their populations plummet to zero as people feared being located in possible target zones. Everyone in the country seems to be headed toward middle-America. There is a rumor of a place that is safe from attacks."

"Oh my God," Elle gasped. "No wonder this place looks like it was abandoned in a hurry."

After several hours of reading and searching for more answers, Hayden suggested they call it a night. Elle readily agreed. As they passed a campus restaurant, Hayden used his powers to melt through the lock on the exterior door. Once inside, they rummaged through the kitchen area in search of a meal.

"Looks like people grabbed some stuff, but there is still plenty here to eat and drink," Hayden observed. "The majority of it is still good, too. Let's eat real quick before we find a place to spend the night."

After their meal, Hayden and Elle wandered until they came across a student residential area. They walked up to one of the buildings that had the exterior doors propped open. As they walked through the building, Hayden listened intently for any signs of activity. Not surprisingly, no one else was in the building. They made their way up to the third floor and found a decent-looking apartment-style room.

"I guess this one looks as good as any," Hayden said. "What do you think?"

"Yeah, it's nice enough," Elle agreed.

After looking around and finding a lack of supplies in the room, Hayden explored several other rooms on the floor. It appeared that the prior residents took most of what they could carry when they left. He gathered essentials from the rooms and broke into a vending machine for water and snacks.

"We will have to bring some food and water back with us tomorrow," Hayden told Elle as he entered the room.

"Okay, hopefully, we won't be here too long before you figure out how to get us back," she replied.

"I agree. I'll get us back as quickly as I can."

They walked through the floorplan together. Other than the kitchen and living room, they found two single rooms, one double room, and a bathroom. The rooms were still adorned with posters, lamps, and textbooks.

"We should probably get some sleep so we can wake up early and continue the research," Hayden suggested. "I'm sure you're just as exhausted as I am."

"I am exhausted. Honestly, I don't even know how I'm still awake," Elle admitted. "Not to give away the fact that I'm totally scared, but are you okay with us sharing that bigger room with two beds? I really don't want to be alone. This entire place, the entire city, is just really creepy because it's so empty... but I'm still afraid that someone is going to find us and attack us."

"Yeah, of course, we can do that," Hayden told her. "I completely get what you're saying. There is a really spooky vibe in this town. I've never seen it with zero people before."

"Okay, thank you," Elle replied. "I'll try to find some blankets for the beds."

Hayden nodded in acknowledgment. "I'll go lock the door and grab some water bottles for us."

After securing the room, Hayden turned the lights off and settled into the twin-size bed along the wall opposite the bed Elle had chosen for herself. "Goodnight."

"Goodnight," Elle replied, her voice soft and faint from drowsiness already beginning to wash over her.

∾ ∾ ∾ ∾ ∾ ∾

The next morning, Elle woke up and looked over to see that Hayden was already out of his bed. She anxiously wandered into the living room and found him there. On the kitchen counter sat fresh clothes and a pile of breakfast junk foods.

"I was really quick," Hayden said. "I flew over to the college's bookstore and got us both a change of clothes. There's a T-shirt and sweatpants on the counter for you. It's a little cold outside, so there's a hoodie up there also… new socks, too. The only thing they didn't carry was underwear, so we might have to go out somewhere later if we're going to be here a while."

"You remembered my sizes," Elle replied as she looked at the tags.

"Was I supposed to forget them?" Hayden joked.

No, I was just making an observation," Elle said and laughed. "Well, as long as these sweatpants are comfy, then who needs underwear."

"Touché. It's not like we're putting on a fashion show here," Hayden agreed as he stood and jokingly modeled his head-to-toe UCSD emblazoned outfit. "I already showered, so it's all yours. This place still has hot water, that's a definite plus. I *borrowed* you a new towel and a hairbrush from the bookstore also."

"Thank you," Elle responded as she grabbed a package of mini-donuts from the counter, along with her new clothes.

As Elle waited for the water to warm in the shower, she snacked on the donuts and looked at herself in the mirror. Upon observing just how dirty her clothes were from the previous day, Elle was thankful that Hayden had gone out to get replacements. Grey dust from the other planet, dried sweat, and speckles of blood were seemingly embedded in the fabric of everything, even her undergarments.

"Wow, this is not cute," Elle said aloud to herself as she undressed.

After enjoying the warmth of the shower water washing over her aching muscles, Elle finally stepped out. After a quick glimpse in the mirror, she proceeded to brush her hair out and get dressed.

"I didn't even notice how disgusting my clothes were," she told Hayden as she walked back into the living room. "They all went straight into the trash. So shopping may be on the agenda after all."

"Well, cross your fingers that we get out of here today," Hayden said. "Otherwise, we'll stock up on supplies."

Throughout the day, Hayden went back and forth between papers and articles on the computer. He gleaned some useful information, but as the evening came, he found that he was still far from a solution. After they stopped back in at the restaurant for dinner, Hayden told Elle that they were going to make a quick detour before heading to the residence hall.

"Campus police?" Elle asked as they approached the building.

As they walked inside and down the main corridor, Hayden spotted the supply area.

"Just in case," Hayden told her as he handed her a handgun and several boxes of spare ammunition. "I want you to be able to protect yourself in case something happens to me."

"Nothing better happen to you!" Elle protested as she placed the items in her backpack.

Hayden grabbed two police radios and chargers from the supply closet and put them into the backpack as well. "Communication, in case we are apart."

The sun was setting as they arrived back at the residence hall. Once inside, Hayden found a pen and paper to compile a list of needed supplies.

"Do you think I would be safe here alone?" Elle asked. "I'm a little worried about going out somewhere new in the dark."

"Yeah, I think you'll be okay," Hayden replied. "I'm fairly certain the entire city is empty. I'll take one of the radios. If you need me to come back for any reason, just let me know, and I'll be here in a few seconds."

"Okay," Elle agreed.

"So, let's get a shopping list done," Hayden suggested. "I'm definitely getting us some toothbrushes and toothpaste. Like you said this morning, I still know your sizes, so I'll get you some more clothes, bras, and underwear. I will try to get as much food as I can carry. What else?"

"Shampoo, conditioner, and soap," Elle added. "The stuff that was in the shower is almost gone. That's the only essential things that I can think of."

"Okay, I think that's a good list. Shouldn't be too much to carry back."

"Ohh, wait a sec," Elle said abruptly, with a look on her face that communicated she was trying to figure something out. She got up and slowly ran around the corner into the bathroom for a moment before reemerging. As she walked back into the front room, she huffed in displeasure. "Do you mind getting me a box of tampons also? Apparently, I just started my period."

"Yeah, of course I will," Hayden replied and added it to the list. "I'll head out right now, and I'll try to be back in like fifteen minutes. Remember, call me on the radio if you need anything."

Elle held up her radio to acknowledge Hayden's request. "Thank you."

Hayden set out to gather supplies. Once he reached the residence hall courtyard, he took off in flight. Seconds later, he arrived at the nearest store and walked inside. He was surprised to see the place mostly intact. Evidently, people were in such a hurry to leave the area that almost no looting occurred. As he walked past the registers, Hayden grabbed a handful of shopping bags and quickly reviewed the list again. He made a mad dash through the store, collecting everything.

Sixteen minutes later, Hayden arrived back at the residence hall and walked into the apartment with shopping bags spanning the length of both his forearms. Elle was reclined on the couch. "Trying to fly with all of this is certainly a workout," he joked as he set the bags on the dining room table.

Before unloading anything else, Hayden briefly rummaged through the shopping bags and pulled out the box of tampons and a package of flushable wet wipes.

"Thank you!" Elle effused gratitude as Hayden handed her the packages. As she headed to the bathroom, Hayden began to empty the other shopping bags.

"Hayden!" Elle called out from the bathroom.

"What's up?" he asked in a raised voice.

"Ummm, so I don't know how I forgot this, but can you bring me some underwear and pants? I am not putting these sweatpants back on."

"Yeah, give me a second to find them," Hayden said while chuckling. He grabbed a pair of fleece shorts and a pair of panties and proceeded down the hallway, stopping just short of the bathroom door. Hayden reached around the door frame with the clothing items in his hand.

"Thank you," Elle said in a hushed voice as she took the clothes.

Hayden returned to the dining room and continued unpacking the grocery bags. A minute later, Elle appeared back in the dining room.

"These shorts are so soft. I am literally in love with them," she said.

"Glad you like them," Hayden replied. "Go ahead and relax. I'll put all this stuff away."

"Are you sure?'

"Yeah, I got it. Relax, Elle."

She reluctantly obliged and headed over to the front room to sit on the couch.

"Oh my God, Hayden…" Elle said as she rounded the corner. "Are you trying to win an award or something?"

"No, I'm just trying to take care of you," Hayden replied. "I just added a few things to the list that I thought you might want or need."

Elle appeared back in front of Hayden. Her hands were on her hips in a display of feigned shock. She began listing the items Hayden had bought and placed on the coffee table for her.

"Pain relievers, dark chocolate, a heating pad, my

favorite tea, and a book that hasn't even come out yet in our time. How do you even remember what my favorite tea is?"

"You act like I don't pay attention," Hayden said, laughing.

"Thank you so much," Elle said. "Lots of people only do the bare minimum, if that. You always go out of your way to do more than is expected."

"You're welcome," Hayden replied. "I'm just about done putting all this away. Hopefully tomorrow we can find some answers."

℘ ℘ ℘ ℘ ℘ ℘

Hayden and Elle woke up early and headed back to the physics building to continue their research. Hours of grueling searching were beginning to wear on their determination.

"I think I finally found something," Hayden told her with newfound hope in his voice.

"What is it?" Elle asked as she scooted her chair closer to Hayden's.

"This professor published a paper in October 2026 about his work with a joint research program between CERN and NASA on micro-singularities."

"Can that help us?" Elle asked enthusiastically.

"Well, getting to the results and data section, I don't know," Hayden replied. "The results of the experiments were inconclusive. We'll set this paper aside in case we need it. Let's keep looking."

The day waned on into the evening, and the duo repeated their routine of getting dinner at the campus restaurant and retiring for the night in the residence hall.

As they lay in their separate beds preparing for sleep, Elle vocalized her worries to Hayden.

"Are we ever going to get out of here?" she asked. "I do trust you and everything. It just seems like we're never going to find anything that will help us. Thinking about being here in an abandoned future for months or years is frightening."

"I know how you feel," Hayden sympathized. "I don't blame you for feeling doubt or worry. This does seem like an impossible task, but we will get out of here. I promised you that we would, and I don't intend to break that promise. We just have to keep our hopes high in the meantime. Tomorrow, let's do a half-day of research and take the afternoon off to go out, relax, and clear our heads."

"I like that idea," Elle agreed as she snacked on a couple bites of chocolate.

ひつ ひつ ひつ ひつ ひつ ひつ

After spending the morning in the computer lab, Hayden and Elle set off for Mission Bay. Strolling into the deserted yacht club, Hayden located the keys to a boat docked in the marina.

Elle lay in the open bow of the boat, taking in what sun she could on the mid-February day, while Hayden leisurely navigated around the bay. They docked at several points to explore the desolate resorts, campgrounds, and parks.

"Hungry?" Hayden asked Elle as dusk started to approach.

"Yes!" she replied. "Can we try to find something over here and take a break from the food at the university?"

"Of course."

They came upon a small taco shop along Mission Boulevard that still had power. Hayden perused through the walk-in fridge and found some ingredients that hadn't expired yet. Elle sat on a barstool and whimsically sang while Hayden lit the grill and made tacos.

"This smells delicious," Elle said as Hayden slid her plate across the counter.

"Well, let's hope it tastes as good as it smells," Hayden joked as he sat on the barstool beside Elle with his plate.

"It does," Elle confirmed, nodding and speaking through a mouthful of food.

After their meal, Hayden and Elle walked north along Mission Boulevard until they reached Reed Avenue. At Elle's request, they headed west to the sands of Pacific Beach.

"Take your shoes off and walk along the water with me," Elle insisted as they hopped over the boardwalk seawall.

Hayden did as instructed, and they walked along the coast, passing underneath Crystal Pier and continuing until the Law Street beach ramp.

"If we're still trapped here in a month, we are definitely moving to one of these houses," Elle joked as they reached the neighborhood at the top of the ramp.

"You got yourself a deal," Hayden replied. "Might as well live in style if we're stuck here for too long."

"Thank you for taking me out today," Elle said. "I think we both really needed the break."

"We definitely did," Hayden agreed. "Minus the apparent apocalypse in this time, having the town to ourselves was really relaxing. Are you ready to head back?"

Elle nodded in affirmation, and they made the short flight back to the university.

ɔ ɔ ɔ ɔ ɔ ɔ

The next nine days passed with minimal progress. Though

Elle and Hayden found several articles and research papers that they thought might be useful, their hopes were dashed each time when Hayden began making calculations. In an effort to maintain their sanity, they began venturing outside the campus every other day.

While Elle relaxed on the couch in the residence hall apartment, Hayden sat across from her on the recliner chair, deep in thought. He was distraught by how little progress he had achieved in fulfilling his promise to get them back to the present. With all of the powers that he had at his disposal, he couldn't help feeling powerless.

Outside the window, a thunderstorm was slowly passing through the city. Droplets of water pelted the glass and thunder rolled in the distance. The smell of rain would occasionally bring Hayden out of his contemplative state and back into the moment.

"What are you thinking about?" Elle asked him as she closed her book.

"I'm just trying to figure out what it is that I'm missing," Hayden replied.

"Well, let's brainstorm together," Elle suggested, trying to encourage him. "If only there was someone that we could ask for help."

"There actually might be someone," Hayden's voice

perked up slightly.

"Who?"

"This is going to sound slightly crazy," Hayden warned. "That alien creature that tried to destroy Earth... when I defeated it, my amulet received a blast of its remaining power. Somehow, inside the dreamscape, the creature's collection of memories lives on. It spoke to me once before and warned me about Kali. Maybe it has some answers."

"Can you trust it?"

"I don't know," Hayden admitted. "I didn't at first when it said that Kali was corrupted. However, it was telling the truth. I think that it's worth a shot."

"Okay. While you go into the dreamscape, I'll stay awake and keep watch," Elle said. "I guess it's my turn to protect you now."

"I'll come back as quickly as possible," Hayden assured Elle as he settled himself into the chair.

Hayden closed his eyes and reopened them to the dreamscape. He hadn't bothered to fill the space with a visually pleasing landscape. All that surrounded him was an endless open field lit with a gentle morning sun. Immediately, he called out to the orb. It obliged his call and appeared in front of him.

"I need your help," Hayden said, wasting no time on

small talk.

"You think that I will help you?" the orb responded.

"Yes, I do. You warned me about Kali, and you were right."

"What is your problem?" the orb asked.

"Kali pulled me and another person into a portal. I fought her on another planet. It went sideways, but she ended up portalling out of there. The problem is that the planet was near a massive black hole. When we left, time dilation resulted in us returning to Earth in the year 2027. We need to get back."

"So you're looking for time travel?"

"I guess so," Hayden replied. "We've been searching for a scientific answer, but nothing is ultimately helpful."

"I will help you because you were a worthy opponent, and for that, I respect you," the orb admitted. "My species was advanced. However, we were not so advanced that we mastered time travel. We came up with a rudimentary system to complete the process. However, it is not instantaneous and comes with risks and variances. If it weren't for your level of power, the process would easily kill you. It may, anyway."

"I'm willing to risk it," Hayden said. "How do I do this process?"

"I do not know it completely by memory," the orb

replied. "However, the instructions are on a tablet locked inside a container I brought to Earth long ago. You will have to retrieve and open the container to learn the process."

"Okay, where is it, and how do I open it?"

"It is buried eighty feet underground. The location is on the outskirts of a town that is now known as al-Mayadin in Syria. Go to the farmland at the coordinates 35.001826, 40.444129, and dig there. The container can only be opened by my species. Luckily, your amulet will work to open it. Once you have the tablet, come back to me here and I will tell you how to use it."

"Okay, I can do that," Hayden confirmed.

As he concluded his conversation with the orb, Hayden noticed severe anomalies in the fabric of the dreamscape. The simple field that spanned in all directions glitched with bright colors, and the artificial sun flickered like a lightbulb on its last gasps of life. Hayden looked around for a moment, confused by the abnormalities.

"Elle!" Hayden muttered as his mind changed from idle confusion to sudden panic with the realization that something must be wrong in the real world.

☙ ☙ ☙ ☙ ☙ ☙

"...will enjoy taking you with us," an unknown voice registered in Hayden's ears as he began to open his eyes back to reality.

"Hayden!" Elle's pitched scream was cracked with an overwhelming terror.

As his eyes sprung open, Hayden observed two men in the room. They were both dressed raggedly and stunk of alcohol. One of them appeared to be keeping watch and held the handgun that Elle had left on the kitchen counter. The other man lurched over Elle with his hands wrapped around her ankles as he attempted to pry her from the couch.

"Let go of the damn couch," the man demanded. "If you don't stop resisting, then we're going to make the rest of the night extremely horrific for you."

Hayden stood from the chair in a sudden, fluid motion. The man keeping watch reacted by swinging the handgun over in Hayden's direction. Before the bandit was able to get a shot off, Hayden sent the weapon flying across the room with a powerful gust of directed air.

"What the hell?" the man yelled in surprise, then readied himself to rush Hayden. "You're still going to die!"

Elle's eyes met Hayden's for a brief moment before she diverted her glance downward. She watched as the symbol of Fire emblazoned the back of both his hands. The man on lookout duty took two steps toward Hayden before suddenly stopping again. Hayden clenched his fists closed. The man screamed out in horrifying pain as his bones lit ablaze in his body. Elle looked away as the bandit's skin and muscle began to peel from the bone. His screams faltered and faded as his body was reduced to nothing more than smoldering goo on the wood floor of the apartment. The pungent scent of burnt flesh filled the air.

The second man's grip on Elle's ankles released immediately upon seeing the demise of his partner. He sprinted toward the door, seeking escape, but failed to reach it before Hayden used his powers to slam it shut. The bandit backed up against the door and began to stammer unintelligibly as Hayden walked toward him.

"I… I'm… I'll go… She… I… Didn't touch," he attempted to form a coherent sentence in an appeal for his life.

"You what?" Hayden snarled back at him. "I know damn well what you and your friends would have done to her. Plead all you want, but you'll find no forgiveness here. Not when you threaten her."

The bandit's words turned into punctuated gasps for air as he hyperventilated in fear. Hayden raised a hand, and the glass windows behind him shattered into a thousand pieces. The fragments momentarily floated in the air before

Hayden sent them flying at the man with immense speed. The blood spatter sprayed out across the dining room as the shards made impact. Hayden turned around and dashed over to Elle.

"Are you okay?" he asked as Elle wrapped her arms around him and buried her face against his shoulder.

"I'm alright," she replied as she continued to sob. "Thank you for saving me."

"Elle, I'm very happy that you're okay," Hayden started. "But it was my fault that anyone even had the chance to do that. I should have made sure your gun was by you before I went into the dreamscape. I should have brought up a forcefield around you before I went in. I got way too complacent and comfortable, thinking that no one else was in this city. I know better."

"It's not your fault," Elle insisted. "We haven't seen a single person in over a week, and we've been all over the city."

"I still failed at keeping you safe," Hayden replied. "I'm sorry for that. Who knows if those two guys were alone or if there are others. Anyway, I learned what we need to do to get out of here."

"You did?" Elle asked, her voice now more hopeful.

"We need to take a trip to a town in Syria and find a tablet that's buried underground. Apparently, there is some secret alien time-travel hack that will get us back to our time. Looks like it's time to move out of here anyway."

"Yeah, this place was nice while it lasted, but I'm ready to go. I'll start packing some essentials into my backpack. I'll try to keep it light."

"Go ahead and pack anything you want to keep. I'm not going to make you endure flying that long. We'll just portal there. There's no evidence, so far, that Kali is still in this time period. Even if she is, she's probably not actively tracking my portals. It's been years for her since she saw us last. Regardless, we won't stay in one place for too long."

Elle came back to the front room ten minutes later with her backpack full of her and Hayden's things. After taking one last look around the apartment, Hayden opened a portal, and they stepped into it.

ඏ ඏ ඏ ඏ ඏ ඏ

The other end of the portal tore open near the town of al-Mayadin. Upon stepping out, Hayden looked around and noticed that the city also showed evidence of mass migration from Kali's attacks. They stood in the middle of a large agricultural area that had been untended for several months. The morning sun still hung low in the eastern sky.

"This is the place," Hayden told Elle. "Now I just have to dig down about eighty feet."

Hayden activated the powers of Air and Earth. The ground beneath them began to rumble, and a torrent of soil flew up into the air, dispersing across the surrounding field. Elle looked on in wonder at the dirt pouring down like rain. Within a few seconds, Hayden had reached his desired depth and peered down into the hole he had created. He activated the power of Light and directed a beam into the hole, illuminating a matte grey object that glimmered slightly when the light hit it. Once again, using the power of Air, Hayden levitated the object from the depths to the surface.

"Do you hear that?" Elle asked him. "It sounds like vehicles."

"Yeah, I do," Hayden agreed. "That little show must have drawn the attention of some people still around here. Let's get the tablet out of here and go."

Hayden took the amulet from around his neck and pressed it against the case. Almost instantly, the material started to react to the orange stone. The top of the case sprung open, and a single tablet of black stone sat inside. Hayden was surprised at how light it was compared to its appearance as he picked it up. The sound of multiple vehicles drew closer, and Elle pointed out a trail of dust rising from a nearby road.

"Let's go," Hayden told her as he opened a new portal.

"Where are we now?" Elle asked as they walked through the other end of the portal into an unfamiliar landscape. The snow crunched beneath their shoes, and a bitter wind streaked through the bare branches of trees lining the road.

"A little town called Shullsburg in Wisconsin," Hayden told her. "This ought to be out of the way enough to be safe for the night."

The dead silence of the town was broken as Elle pushed open the front door of an abandoned home. The hinges creaked in protest to their entry after enjoying months of dormancy. Hayden immediately located a pile of wood in the front room and lit the fireplace. They barricaded the doors and windows of the living room to help prevent another surprise attack like the one in San Diego.

"Let's sleep for now. It's been a very long day," Hayden suggested. "We can spend tomorrow figuring out how to use that tablet."

℘ ℘ ℘ ℘ ℘ ℘

Elle and Hayden slept in until almost noon the next morning. Elle awoke to Hayden sitting on the recliner he had utilized as a bed, leaving her the comfort of the larger sofa. He was rummaging through the backpack for snacks that would serve as their breakfast. The warmth on Elle's face told her that Hayden had been up long enough to add more fuel to the fireplace.

"Good morning," Hayden said as he tossed a bag of powdered donuts to Elle. "Let's eat and then head into the dreamscape."

Elle ate her breakfast while Hayden went around the room, making sure that there were no signs of anyone attempting to break in overnight. Once satisfied with the house's security, Hayden laid a plush blanket in the corner of the room and gathered their belongings there. When she was ready to go, Elle joined Hayden in the corner of the room.

"We'll just lay back on this blanket while we enter the dreamscape," Hayden told her. "This time, I'm going to make sure we are much better protected."

Elle sat down, and Hayden cast a forcefield around them. He then activated the powers of Light and Darkness, which he focused on the forcefield. The streams of energy fused with the sphere, complimenting each other perfectly to create an effect of invisibility. Finally, he sat down next to Elle and held the alien tablet in his hand.

"Time for some answers," he told her. "Let's figure out

how to get back home."

Hayden pulled them both into the dreamscape. Once again, the simple landscape was free of frills and the exquisite beauty that Hayden had created in the past. Elle stood next to Hayden and looked around the oddly generic field while he called out to the orb.

"I am here," the orb said as it appeared.

"I have the tablet," Hayden told it. "What do I do now?"

"Who is this?" the orb asked as Elle stared at the floating ball of light.

"This is Elle," Hayden responded.

"You will have to tap the limits of your power if you are thinking about taking her back with you," the orb advised.

"I am prepared to do so," Hayden advised.

"Show me the tablet," the orb instructed.

Hayden held the tablet out in his hand. It was covered with symbols from another language.

"Hold the amulet in your palm and touch the tablet," the orb continued. "Then utter the words Obsequim Delevante Revelus."

Hayden did as he was told. The writing on the tablet began to glow. Each etched letter appeared to swirl with an almost fire-like orange hue. Hayden felt a rush of knowledge surge through his mind.

"Now you know the process needed to attempt a journey back to your time," the orb told him. "You will need to open the first portal just outside a black hole. The one near the planet Kali brought you to should suffice. You will need to be absolutely sure that you take every precaution to protect your bodies for the trip. The calculations you make before opening the portal must be precise, or you could end up at a point in time you did not intend."

"Thank you," Hayden said to the orb. "Is there anything else I need to know?"

"Guard your minds," the orb added. "Even some of my species have come out the other end with nothing more than a mush of insanity and chaos. Set a trigger on your forcefield so that you'll awaken once you reach the other side."

"Alright, then it's time to do this," Hayden said.

"You have unlocked a great deal of power by fashioning and mastering that amulet," the orb added. "Because I respect your ability to harness so much power and defeat me, I will unlock the remaining power in the stone. It will enhance your abilities tenfold."

"Thank you," Hayden responded. "Farewell, for now."

Elle and Hayden woke up on the blanket in the corner of the Wisconsin home. Looking around, nothing seemed to be disturbed. The fireplace was extinguished, and cold had begun invading the room again. As Elle sat up, she shivered through her hoodie.

"How long were we out for? It's freezing in here," Elle asked.

"Apparently, a few hours," Hayden guessed.

As Elle walked over and sat on the sofa, Hayden took the blanket from the floor and placed it over her shoulders before adding new wood to the fireplace and relighting it. Once the heat began radiating through the living room again, Hayden took a seat next to Elle and grabbed a pencil and pad of paper from the coffee table.

"So this is a pretty complex calculation to do in order to pull off this process," Hayden told her as he pulled a stack of research papers and charts they had taken from San Diego out of the backpack. "I'll need to calculate the coordinates of where we will begin the trip, where we want to come out on the other side, their relation to each other in the universe, expected gravitational forces, and several other factors."

"Well, I believe in you," Elle reassured him.

Six hours later, Hayden had filled several sheets of paper with equations and calculations. Elle watched intently as he worked, only taking breaks to add more wood to the fireplace. After shuffling through the stack of notes to double-check his work, Hayden finally stood and stretched his legs.

"I think we're ready," he told Elle with a cautious optimism in his voice.

"For as scary and horrific as this future has been at times, it had its moments," Elle said as she stood. "Moments that I guess I could label as happiness or even contentment. Either way, I'm happy that you were here with me."

"Same, Elle," Hayden concurred. "You gave me a reason to keep on fighting to get back home. Are you ready to go back?"

"Definitely! Your apartment beats abandoned dorms and frozen cities any day of the week."

After gathering their things, Hayden opened a portal in the front room and led Elle through it.

༐ ༐ ༐ ༐ ༐ ༐

A bright orange flash from Hayden's portal appeared in the darkness of space near the black hole. His powers kicked in immediately to provide Elle and himself with protection, air, and heat. They both stared in awe at the enormity and fear-inducing beauty of what was before them.

"I will have the next portal ready soon," Hayden

advised Elle.

Hayden closed his eyes and concentrated on the gateway he intended to make while chanting language from the alien tablet. Eight minutes later, a portal swirled open, closer to the event horizon. It radiated brightly through the entire spectrum of colors, unlike anything Hayden had ever seen.

"Now, to create a forcefield strong enough to keep us alive," Hayden continued his narration of the steps he was taking.

Beginning with a normal Chantiatus field, Hayden grasped the amulet and pulled from the depths of his powers. The symbols of power flashed in sequence on the back of his hands. The amulet let off such brilliant light that it startled Elle. Hayden touched his palms against the forcefield, and a surge of energy flowed into it. Hayden touched the amulet against the fortified barrier to create a trigger that would wake them when they exited the other side of the gateway.

"One last thing before we go," Hayden said as he looked at Elle. "This journey is going to take two years to complete. In order for our bodies to survive the trip, I am going to chant a spell from that tablet that will essentially put us into a state of suspended animation. As that happens,

I'm going to send our minds into the dreamscape. In order to conserve energy, it will be a very basic construct. It will pretty much just be a tiny room, only furnished with two chairs. You and I will not be able to get up and move around, but we will be able to see each other and communicate. Basically, our bodies will be frozen stiff, but our minds will be alive and linked to each other."

"Will it hurt or be uncomfortable in the dreamscape, not being able to move?" Elle asked, the concern evident in her voice.

"No," Hayden replied. "The construct is still what I make of it. I'm going to eliminate our minds' perception of pain, discomfort, restlessness, and all of that."

"Okay, as long as we can still talk to each other in there," Elle said, now slightly more relaxed.

Hayden sighed heavily and focused. As Hayden began to chant, wisps of light swirled in front of them, seemingly laying out a path from their position to the portal.

"Palkischus Abradyschnavya Capseevaye," Hayden began the spell from the tablet. "Phohkraaste Infimitum."

Excruciatingly bright light seared the space around the forcefield. Elle felt a terrifying wave of darkness wash over her mind and a chill that seemed to freeze every inch of her body to the bone. She looked over at Hayden as she lost control of her body. As they fell, he reached out and placed his hand on her forehead. Their bodies collapsed neatly next to each other as their minds flashed into the dreamscape. Hayden and Elle's bodies sped into the new portal. As they entered, a streak of light tore from the back of the portal and disappeared into the black hole.

Nine minutes and fifty-two seconds after they had arrived in space, they were gone.

أميرة الدهر

Chapter Seven

Amira al-Dahr

"How long has it been?" Elle asked.

"It must be close to two years now," Hayden told her. "Time is so hard to keep track of in the dreamscape."

"You know, as much as I feared this just before you cast that last spell, being in this place with you has been... peaceful."

"It really has been," Hayden agreed. "No apocalypses, no fighting, no stress... just peace and sharing thoughts between one another."

"Do you remember," Elle started. "That time you randomly came by my family's house three years ago. I guess you were just passing through town because you didn't stay long and seemed like you were in a rush. What you told me right before you left is what I want to tell you now."

"Three years ago?" Hayden asked. "So, like 2020? Other than your birthday last year, I haven't been up to your house since 2019… right before I started college at Fullerton."

"You don't remember coming by in 2020?" Elle replied. "Maybe it will refresh your memory when I tell you what you said to me. I…"

The portal opened five hundred feet above the Pacific Ocean, nearly eight miles off the coast of Southern California. Hayden and Elle fell through it and hurtled toward the water. The sensory trigger cast on the forcefield sent a shock to the amulet, and they woke suddenly. Hayden grabbed ahold of Elle and took flight, heading westward.

After several minutes, Hayden and Elle landed outside Armond's home and walked up the brick path toward the front door. Armond, seeing them from a window, opened the door to greet them.

"Hayden, where have you been?" Armond forcefully inquired.

"Long story," Hayden replied. "What date is it, Armond?"

"What date?" Armond said, confused. "It's June 22nd… no one has seen you in over four months!"

"Oh my God…" Hayden replied. "I must have

miscalculated."

"Miscalculated what?" Armond insisted. "Where have you been? People think you kidnapped Elle and ran off."

"What the fuck…" Hayden said in disbelief. "Is everything alright? Has Kali been back?"

"No, we haven't seen her at all," Armond replied.

"Ten minutes," Elle interrupted. "We were outside the black hole for about ten minutes before we started the journey back here. Did you include that time dilation effect in your calculations?"

"That is exactly what happened!" Hayden exclaimed, realizing that Elle was precisely correct. "Two hours on that planet was four years on Earth. Ten minutes in the gravitational field would equal about four months."

"Okay, now I'm baffled," Armond admitted. "But regardless, where have you been?"

Hayden sighed as he prepared to tell Armond what had happened. "Kali pulled Elle and me through a portal to another planet. I managed to hold her off during the fight, but she injured me. Once I recovered, Elle and I went back to Earth, but it was desolate. We discovered that the planet Kali took us to was near a supermassive black hole, and the time dilation from its gravitational field had us stuck four years in the future."

"Wait… what?" Armond was visibly shocked by the revelation.

"We eventually found a way to use the amulet to bring us backward in time, but Elle and I have spent the last… well, two years and four months traveling back here."

"I don't understand. The two of you look exactly the same as when I last saw you…" Armond replied. "Neither of you have aged at all."

"I put our bodies in a sort of suspended animation state to survive the trip. We haven't physically aged, but our minds were alive and active inside the dreamscape. We spent the last couple of years making the journey together inside a construct."

"Hayden, that's incredible," Armond mused aloud. "Although you may have some trouble trying to explain that to the detectives that are looking for Elle. They think she's been kidnapped. I don't think that the time travel explanation is going to help you disprove that in their eyes."

"I don't give a shit about that, Armond," Hayden interjected. "We've got more important things to worry about right now."

"I agree," Armond replied. "But just so you're aware, this has been circulating for about nine weeks now."

Armond held up a small poster that showed both

Hayden and Elle's pictures, along with a "wanted for questioning" headline and details about a possible abduction. Hayden and Elle briefly observed the details.

Hayden snapped his fingers and pointed them at the poster, lighting it on fire. Armond threw the poster to the ground and stamped it out.

"Like I said, I'll deal with that if I have to," Hayden added. "I'm not worried about it. Let's all meet up here tomorrow morning so I can fill everyone else in, and then we can discuss what happens next. I have a feeling that Kali will reappear soon now that I'm back."

Armond nodded his head in agreement. Hayden and Elle took flight again and traveled back to Hayden's apartment. Hayden landed on the back patio to avoid any potential interactions with neighbors, and he and Elle walked inside. Other than some dust, everything appeared to be the same.

"Elle, I'm going to head over to Dan's for just a couple minutes. Stay here and don't go outside, alright?" Hayden said.

"Okay, be safe… and don't be gone too long!" Elle replied.

Hayden shot her a smile and nodded. He then walked out to the back patio and disappeared into the sky.

Elle looked around the apartment. It appeared that their friends had cleaned out the refrigerator and several cupboards. She was thankful they hadn't returned to the smell of rotten and moldy food. Elle tossed a dust-covered hand towel that had been on the kitchen counter into the laundry room. While walking toward the hallway, she decided to wait until later to compile a shopping list. She made her way to the bathroom and looked at herself in the mirror.

"Armond was right," she thought, "I look exactly the same… but I feel like I haven't showered in years."

Elle reached into the shower and turned it on. As the water warmed, she took each piece of her clothing off… again observing herself in the mirror, noticing that her physical appearance hadn't changed at all. Her hair was the exact same length, her makeup still mostly intact, her body the same size… as if she had simply just dozed off that fateful night, had a bad dream, and woke up the next morning. Her mind felt slightly disconnected from the reality that was the present.

She stepped into the now steaming shower and stood in the water, enjoying the feeling. As she washed herself and shaved her body, she recounted her time stuck in San Diego. Elle wondered if Hayden would be surprised once he looked in a mirror. Eventually, her mind wandered to the long journey within the dreamscape back to the present. In the times that she lost track of the passage of time, she had experienced a feeling of uncertainty. She had wondered if they would be stuck inside that dark, inhospitable construct forever. However, she was grateful that she never felt lonely. Even when days blurred into months, Hayden had been there. They constantly communicated. Each of them told the other their life stories. Not just the surface story, not just the parts that they already knew... the uncountable minutes allowed for the conveyance of their childhoods, their feelings, their fears.

There had come a time for Elle, which she guessed was a couple months ago, that her mind marked as a turning point. She had always appreciated everything that Hayden had done for her. They had always shared a jovial relationship. Her mind pivoted back to 2020 and she wondered if Hayden had known something then, that she didn't realize until now. Whatever the particulars were, she decided that she was going to act.

ℭ ℭ ℭ ℭ ℭ ℭ

"You missed the graduation ceremony," Dan told Hayden. "I talked to Professor Alvarez and convinced him you were out saving the world again. He definitely thinks highly of you,

I'll say that. He just went ahead and gave you an 'A' in the class. I also logged into your student portal and made sure you were all set to graduate. I gave your degree to your parents. They came down for the ceremony, and Abby and I kept them company. You should definitely go see them soon. Also, everything is all set for the fall quarter at UCI."

"I cannot thank you enough," Hayden told Dan. "I definitely owe you. Tomorrow, I'll explain everything that happened while I was gone."

"You're welcome. You would've done the same for me," Dan said. "I'm just glad you guys are back safe."

Hayden took off in flight back to his apartment. As he casually cut across the sky, Hayden observed the views of the setting sun on the horizon. It lit the cloud-strewn air with brilliantly exploding hues of orange and purple. The scene evoked feelings of calm and contentment in his mind, which replaced the seemingly constant state of worry and uncertainty of the last few years as he and Elle traveled back to the present.

As he continued his journey home, Hayden's mind began to wander. He realized that this was the first time in two years that he had his thoughts completely to himself. The link in the dreamscape between his and Elle's minds had kept them sane throughout the long journey, but it also meant that neither of them had a moment or a thought all to themselves. Hayden hadn't regretted that caveat at all, but he had been looking forward to this moment when he could privately ponder where things stood.

As he relished the moment in flight through the warm evening skies above Fullerton, his mind finally fixated on the thoughts that had been teetering on the edge of his consciousness for the past couple of months. It was now time to confront his feelings.

Hayden quickly recollected the account of events to himself of the past two years. When Kali had drawn him and Elle into her portal, the latter two were no more than friends. Friends whose families had been familiar with each other for a long time. Looking back though, Hayden admitted to himself that they hadn't spent a considerable amount of time alone together. In recent memory, there was just the one day in 2022 while he had spent the weekend at the Hensley's home. Elle had persuaded Hayden to take her to the beach and do some window shopping. Randomly, Hayden realized that he still had the books that Elle had lent to him on that day.

Tragic circumstances had brought them back together. Hayden regretted that he had procrastinated on visiting the family again before the day of the meteorite disaster. Afterward, they had survived a harrowing battle with Kali and endured an almost hopeless search for answers on a near-barren planet. Hayden's efforts to propel them back to the present day came with definite sacrifice. The burden for both of them had been inarguably eased by the fact that they could communicate with each other... throughout what would have otherwise been a tortuous excursion.

Hayden's mind culminated its recap of events to itself. Now, it switched gears to focus on what he actually wanted to delve into. Hayden couldn't deny that over the final few months of their journey back to the present, it seemed that there had been a subtle shift in the relationship between him and Elle. They had become undeniably closer over the years. That was a given, considering they each had unabated access to each other's thoughts. But what Hayden was contemplating now was something more than that. He wondered if their closeness had ignited into something more than just friendship in the past few months. However, he wasn't completely certain, and so he held off on letting those thoughts manifest in his mind, knowing that Elle would have had complete access to them.

Now that he was alone though, the floodgates of his thoughts began to wash over him. Was it possible that in the past couple of months, he had fallen for her? His mind lingered on that question. Eventually, the answer that repeatedly resounded in his head was an undeniable yes.

He pored over every moment of the last few months in his mind, examining all of Elle's interactions with him. His initial feelings had sparked because of something that she had shared in thought with him and the inflection of that thought. It was more whimsical than normal, almost flirtatious, he had thought. The thoughts that they shared with one another after that point began to fall into a pattern, mimicking that same energy.

Hayden considered that perhaps he was wrong. Maybe Elle had simply been in a more elated and hopeful mood, knowing that their journey back to the present was coming close to an end.

"Why am I overthinking this?" Hayden asked himself in slight disbelief at how he was letting his mind run wild.

He had already decided how he felt. He just needed verification that she felt the same way. As his apartment came into view, emotion washed over him. He missed Elle. Despite being together without pause, he felt incredibly lonely after being away from her for a little less than an hour. Hayden felt a sense of desperate longing, even though he would be walking in the door of his apartment in a few seconds and would see her there.

"I suppose that I should bring this up to Elle tonight," Hayden thought as the possibilities cascaded through his thoughts. Despite the inherent threat of Kali attacking at any moment, Hayden's concentration was inward. His thoughts remained fixated, like volcanic ash covers an unsuspecting town the night before a looming disaster. Hayden's feet touched the ground in his front yard as he landed.

As he walked inside and breathed in the refreshingly familiar air of his apartment, Hayden noted the sound of the shower coming from the guest bathroom. He concluded that he too could use some cleaning up. Hayden wandered down the hall and fired up the shower in the master bathroom.

ℂ ℂ ℂ ℂ ℂ ℂ

As Elle stepped out of the shower and began to dry herself off, she heard the shower in the master turn on. "Hayden must be back," she thought to herself.

Elle continued to ready herself in the bathroom. She brushed her teeth and combed out her hair but decided to forgo any makeup as it was now the evening. She found herself contemplating the last twenty-eight months in her mind. After a few minutes, she wrapped her towel back around herself and walked to her bedroom. As she picked out some pajamas, she tossed her towel onto her bed, then slipped on the pair of baby blue shorts and a white cami-style top. She walked out to the kitchen and started to prepare a snack as she heard the shower turn off from the master bathroom.

Elle sat on the couch and ate the bowl of Spaghetti-O's that she had prepared. A few minutes later, Hayden walked down the hallway and into the front room. Elle dipped her spoon into the bowl and then held the spoon up as if motioning for Hayden to take a bite. Hayden gladly obliged, and Elle proceeded to feed him several more spoonfuls, alternating back and forth between Hayden and herself. Elle felt a sense of peace in the moment. They had just spent so much time together, in their minds, but being able to interact physically again... even in such a simple moment, brought her a feeling of joy that she couldn't quite put into words.

After they finished the Spaghetti-O's, Elle washed the bowl out in the kitchen sink and grabbed a bottle of water. Hayden's phone chimed from his bedroom.

"Be right back," he said and walked down the hallway to check who had texted him, but all the while thinking about talking to Elle about how he felt. He decided he would bring it up when he went back to the front room.

As Hayden was finishing up his reply to the text message, Elle appeared in the doorway.

"It was Armond," he informed her. "Just letting me know that everyone is good for tomorrow morning."

Elle didn't respond. She walked over to the side of the bed where Hayden was standing.

"What's up?" Hayden asked her. Elle continued in her stride until she was right in front of him. Hayden looked at her, mildly perplexed at her lack of a response.

Elle placed her hand on Hayden's cheek and leaned in toward him. Her lips met Hayden's. Though he was honestly quite shocked, Hayden kissed her back. After several seconds, she took her lips from his.

"Elle..?" Hayden said, still shocked by what had just happened. Here he was, planning on bringing up his feelings in just a few moments when Elle apparently beat him to the punch... and in an indisputably more direct fashion.

Again, Elle didn't respond. Instead, she reached down to the hem of her shirt and pulled it up and over her head, then tossed it aside. Hayden's surprise was now visibly etched on his face, his mouth slightly agape at the sight of seeing Elle topless for the first time.

"Elle... what..?" Hayden now managed to stammer a

second word.

She continued to hold Hayden's gaze and again remained silent. Elle took a small step back and, after a moment, placed her hands on the waistband of her pajama shorts. Hayden was now effectively speechless.

Elle slid her shorts down over her hips and let them fall to the floor. Hayden didn't even attempt to speak as he looked at Elle, now standing completely nude in front of him. Hayden wasn't sure if it was a few seconds or a few minutes that passed when he heard Elle finally say something.

"Is this weird for you or anything?" Elle asked. "We just spent over two years together. I felt like we were so close, but we couldn't move, and I couldn't feel you next to me. Also, I feel like I haven't changed at all."

Hayden knew exactly what she meant. They had spent so much time together in the dreamscape… bonding, sharing their thoughts, and learning from each other… but she was evidently self-conscious about whether or not that bond would persist. Hayden also noted that, indeed, she looked the same as the day they left San Diego. Hayden shook his head no as if to answer her question nonverbally.

"I love you," were the words that escaped Hayden's lips.

Elle's face beamed with a smile as she stepped toward him. She leaned in and kissed him again. Hayden embraced her as they kissed and fell backward onto the bed. Elle pulled Hayden's shirt up and off him, followed, moments later, by his pajama pants.

Elle rolled over onto her back, and Hayden followed, positioning himself above her. They kissed again, Elle's hands placed on the back of Hayden's neck while one of his hands pressed against her chest. They stopped to take a breath. Elle looked up at Hayden.

"I want to. If you'll have me." As if her words didn't give away her intentions, her eyes glimmered with faint but unmistakable desire.

Hayden didn't say a word, but the look on his face indicated that he understood. He placed his hand on her cheek. The next thirty minutes concluded with Elle and Hayden next to each other on the bed. Elle had nestled her head into his neck, and her body was partially draped over his.

"I love you too. That's exactly it," Elle said as she pulled the comforter up over them. Hayden placed his arm over her and turned off the bedroom light with a voice command to the nearby smart home speaker.

Now exhausted, they quickly fell asleep in each other's arms.

ᔕ ᔕ ᔕ ᔕ ᔕ ᔕ

As the morning sunlight began to peak through the bedroom curtains, Hayden awoke… not to the sound of his alarm, not to birds chirping outside… but to the sound of his front door being kicked in. He sprung up out of bed, waking Elle in the process.

Footsteps rushed down the hallway as Hayden pulled his pajama pants on from the floor beside the bed. Elle, still half asleep and in shock, fell out of the bed and then stumbled to her feet as she quickly dressed herself.

The bedroom door burst open. Hayden was confronted by several police officers with guns and tasers drawn. "Hayden de Vere, you're under arrest for the kidnapping of Elle Hensley," one of the officers barked. As the officer approached, Elle noticed the back of Hayden's palms begin to glow.

"Hayden, don't!" Elle called out to him, recalling what happened in San Diego the last time someone had threatened to take her. "We'll just explain everything that has happened."

Hayden looked back at Elle and then restrained himself, letting the glow from the back of his hands fade away. The officer placed Hayden in handcuffs and led him out the front door to a waiting police cruiser. Another officer instructed Elle that she was taking her to the hospital to meet with a doctor and a social worker.

Hayden stared out the window of the police car, attempting to remain calm in the situation even though he regarded the entire thing as asinine. As they arrived at the police station, an officer led him inside to an interview room. Hayden sat there for several minutes until two detectives walked into the room.

"So Hayden," the first detective started, "I'm Detective Oliver, and this here is my partner, Detective Shillinger."

Oliver was a thirty-something-year-old African-American man who looked like he accidentally got into the line for the police academy on high school career day instead of the Abercrombie model line. His partner, Shillinger, was a late-twenties white female and was equally attractive.

Oliver continued, "I take it you know why you're here, Mr. de Vere."

Hayden resorted to humor. "Yeah, definitely. So where's Ashton at? You guys look like models, not cops. Let me guess, next, Sergeant Channing Tatum is going to walk into the room? This is obviously an episode of Punk'd."

Shillinger held back a laugh, smirking instead. Oliver's demeanor didn't change.

"Let me assure you," Oliver replied. "This is not a prank. You're accused of kidnapping a sixteen-year-old girl,

Elle Hensley. Since our officers found her with you this morning, I would say that there's not a whole lot you can say to refute that charge."

Hayden interrupted. "Kidnapping? Are you kidding? I think you mean saving her life."

"Is that so?" Oliver countered. "She was the only one missing from her home. The rest of her family is dead. You were seen with her on camera footage from several stores in the area immediately after that. Then, instead of bringing her to a hospital or police station to let the proper authorities take care of her, you disappeared with her for four months. If you don't classify that as kidnapping, then I don't know what is."

Shillinger picked up after Oliver concluded. "What were you doing with her for four months? Where did you take her?"

"Okay, first of all," Hayden interjected. "You guys aren't going to understand everything that's happened or where we've been for four months. Also, I went to that house to check on Elle's family after the meteorite disaster. My parents have known her father and mother for a long time. When I got there, the house was in ruins. Elle's brother and mother were already gone. Her father was dying. He made me promise to take her and keep her safe."

"Safe," Shillinger interrupted. "As in take her to the hospital, have her checked out, and let family services get her counseling and find her a safe home. That's safe."

"No, fuck that," Hayden replied. "You think I trust some state agency that'll just end up leaving her traumatized?"

"They're professionals, Mr. de Vere," Oliver interrupted. "You are not. They know what they're doing."

"Not to sound like a total Karen, but do you even know who I am?" Hayden said angrily.

"Yes, we know who you are," Shillinger replied. "And you're not above the law, Mr. de Vere."

"We'll see about that…" Hayden muttered under his breath.

"What was that?" Oliver insisted.

"She wasn't kidnapped!" Hayden raised his voice. "Also, we've been off-world for the past two years and four months, so she's not sixteen either; she's eighteen."

"Oh, could've fooled me," Oliver said. "She looks exactly like her school photo taken a month before you abducted her. Are you trying to earn yourself a mental health hold also? Because you're well on your way to succeeding."

"Oh my God," Hayden replied. "Like I said, you wouldn't understand the truth."

"Well, luckily for you," Oliver responded. "The courts

are still open. Since you haven't told me anything that would negate the charge, we're going to process you and take you before a judge right now."

"Oh, splendid," Hayden replied while rolling his eyes in disbelief at what was happening.

About forty-five minutes later, Hayden was taken into the courthouse near the police station. A public defender introduced himself to Hayden and advised him that he would be handling this initial hearing and what to expect. Elle was seated on a bench in the rear of the courtroom next to a county employee.

They took a seat after the judge entered the courtroom and the assistant district attorney began.

"Your honor," the lawyer started. "The State is charging Mr. de Vere with one count of kidnapping under California Penal Code section 208(b) and one count of child abduction under California Penal Code section 278."

"Thank you," the judge replied, then turned his attention to Hayden and the public defender. "How does your client wish to plead to these charges?"

Hayden stood and replied with growing anger and disgust obviously present in his tone. "Absolutely not guilty to this entire travesty."

The judge replied to the public defender. "Counselor,

can you control your client from making outbursts?"

"Yes, your honor," replied the public defender. "Not guilty is the plea."

"Thank you," the judge continued. "Now for bail, does the State have any requests?"

"Indeed, your honor," the district attorney replied. "Due to the serious nature of these charges and the defendant's flight risk, we request he be held without bail."

The public defender chimed in. "Your honor, that is nonsense. My client is widely regarded as a hero and is well-respected in the community. The State's request is unreasonable."

"Noted," the judge replied. "However, this case is not quite ordinary, so I'm going to rule in favor of the State and order Mr. de Vere to be held without bail until his next hearing, which we can set for July 29th at 9:00 a.m. Additionally, Miss Hensley will be placed into foster care immediately following this hearing."

The public defender began to reply. "Thank yo…"

Hayden rose from his seat again, visibly angry. The bailiff took a cautionary step toward the table where Hayden and the public defender were located.

Hayden turned and looked at Elle, still seated in the back of the courtroom. "I'm sorry, Elle, I tried…" he said to her.

Hayden turned back, now facing the front of the courtroom.

"We are done here," he said in a raised voice. "I am not going to put up with this farcical shit."

The bailiff put his hand on his firearm while the judge yelled across the courtroom. "Mr. de Vere, stand down now! You are being taken back into custody."

"Elle," Hayden called out to her. "We are leaving!" He turned and began to walk toward the back of the courtroom where Elle was now standing.

The judge motioned to the bailiff to stop Hayden. The bailiff advanced and drew his gun as Hayden continued walking toward Elle.

"Stop right now, or I will shoot you!" the bailiff screamed across the room.

"Go ahead," Hayden said flatly and turned back toward the bailiff, who was about twenty feet behind him.

The bailiff, startled, fired two rounds at Hayden. Screams of panic filled the courtroom. Hayden stood in the same position, his arm extended toward the officer with his palm out. The bullets stopped mid-flight in front of Hayden's hand and then fell to the courtroom floor.

"That was a mistake," Hayden said coldly. The back of his hand was now emblazoned with the symbol نار. The bailiff's gun melted in his hands. Everyone in the courtroom was now wide-eyed in panic.

"Anything else?" Hayden yelled across the silence of the courtroom. "Does anyone else want to test my patience?"

The occupants of the courtroom continued to stand where they were, paralyzed with fear.

"Good," Hayden continued. "If y'all insist on pushing me into my Rep Era, then this is what you're going to get. So let me be abundantly clear… do not fuck with me, do not even think about taking Elle from me, and do not get in my way. You will regret it dearly if you do."

Hayden finished walking back to where Elle was standing and took her hand. He led her back up near the front of the courtroom. Hayden raised his hand again, and the back of it glowed with the symbol ةقاط. A shockwave of energy pulsed from Hayden's palm and blew a hole in the courtroom wall, twenty feet in diameter, prompting dozens of people to take shelter behind desks, chairs, and benches.

As Hayden and Elle walked toward their newly made exit, Hayden stopped and patted the public defender on his shoulder. "Thanks for your help," he told the lawyer jokingly. The duo then walked through the gaping hole in the wall to the courtyard outside. Elle wrapped her arms around Hayden, and they disappeared into the sky.

છ છ છ છ છ છ

Hayden and Elle landed a few minutes later at Dan's place, and Hayden walked through the front door without knocking. As he and Elle entered, they found Dan sitting on the couch in his front room, watching the television. It was the local news channel, with a reporter live from outside the courthouse that Hayden and Elle had just come from.

"Bro…" Dan said as he looked over at Hayden. "What did you just do?"

"Ugh," Hayden replied with an exasperated sigh. "I was trying to be civil and explain what happened… but then they fucked around and found out."

"Dude, I was just about to leave for Armond's house when I saw this come on," Dan responded. "Like, you're my best bud. Obviously, I know you're innocent, and whatever's between you and Elle is fine by me… but man, I wouldn't be surprised if SWAT was out looking for you right now."

"Well, thank you for your vote of confidence," Hayden said jokingly. "But you're probably right. Of course, they're not going to heed my warning and leave me alone."

The television report droned on, now interviewing citizens and officials from all over the country about the situation. Everyone was making harsh and damning comments about both Hayden's behavior at the courthouse and his relationship with Elle. Hayden felt his blood begin to boil again.

"Alright, we've gotta get out of here," Hayden told Dan. "Besides, I don't want the SWAT team showing up here on your doorstep. Tell Armond to reschedule the meeting with everyone for 2:00 p.m., and I'll see you there after I take care of a few things."

"Take care of?" Dan questioned.

"Yeah, I'm sure you'll probably see it live on the news," Hayden said with a chuckle. "Plus, I need to get the amulet. They barged into my room this morning and grabbed me before I could get it off the nightstand."

"Alright, man, be safe," Dan replied.

Hayden and Elle walked out the front door of Dan's apartment and took back to the skies, landing moments later on Hayden's back patio. From the air, they could see the police activity moving throughout the city streets. They walked inside and prepared for what was coming.

"Elle, whatever you do, just stay behind me," Hayden instructed her.

"Okay," Elle replied.

Hayden and Elle walked down to his bedroom, where he changed out of the jail clothing and into a pair of jeans and a T-shirt. Hayden grabbed the amulet from the nightstand and placed it around his neck, over his shirt. They then walked down the hallway to Elle's room, and she changed out of her pajamas into leggings and a short-sleeve shirt. Once she was dressed, they made their way out to the front room.

The sounds of multiple vehicles pulling up outside were audible from inside the apartment. Outside, officers urged residents who were outside to either go back inside or flee the area. Several news vans pulled up behind the police barricade. Reporters and camera operators began to set up for what they anticipated to be the story of the week, if not the year.

"Are you ready for this?" Hayden asked Elle. "There's no talking my way out of it this time."

"I'm ready," Elle replied. "Just try not to hurt anyone. They're stupid and wrong, but they've all got families and stuff, Hayden. I don't want anyone dying just because I want to be with you."

Hayden sighed, "Yeah… you're right," he said, then paused. "As long as they don't hurt you because then all bets are off."

Hayden opened the front door and walked outside into the daylight. The news camera operators clamored into position, all attempting to get the best view possible of the unfolding scene. Elle followed out behind Hayden, making sure to remain a few feet behind him.

Hayden observed the grand display of force that had shown up at his doorstep. Armored SWAT vehicles and police cars from departments all over the county were present. Hundreds of officers stood at the ready with shotguns and AR-15 rifles trained on Hayden.

"Surrender now," one of the senior officers demanded over a bullhorn. "Let your hostage go and get on the ground."

Hayden took a few steps forward and could hear the multitude of officers adjusting their weapons to be ready to fire.

"How about this…" Hayden yelled. "I'll give you the chance to surrender right now. Walk away."

As Hayden finished his recommendation, the amulet began to fiercely glow. The words that Hayden had inscribed on the stone began to shine as if they were etched with red-hot fire. Hayden could hear a collective laugh from the throng of officers at his demand that they surrender to him.

"No chance," the officer replied through the bullhorn. "Surrender now, give up the girl, and you'll leave here alive."

Hayden sighed and rolled his eyes as he began to walk forward. He extended his arms out to his side, and for a moment, there was a temporary ease amongst some of the officers who thought it was an indication of surrender.

The back of Hayden's hands both glowed, cycling through the symbols of several different powers... Elle couldn't tell which ones they were because the symbols were going so fast. Hayden continued walking forward.

"No," Hayden simply responded to the officer's demand, now extending his left hand out in front of him.

A deafening chorus of gunfire erupted in the moment. Elle covered her ears and stared on in fear. Hayden's hand stayed outstretched toward the virtual army of police officers. The tension in Elle's body was released when she saw the hundreds, if not thousands of rounds of ammunition fall to the ground in front of Hayden's feet. A collective gasp of disbelief rang out from the crowd.

"Are we done playing around?" Hayden yelled to the stunned officers.

In a state of panic, another round of gunfire erupted. The same conclusion occurred... the sound of spent ammunition ringing out as it fell to the ground in front of Hayden's feet.

"Trying the same thing twice and expecting a different result..." Hayden stated, with a smirk on his face. "Is that not the definition of insanity?"

Hayden heard the sound of footsteps on the roof of his apartment behind him. He looked back to see a dozen officers that had flanked him. Their rifles were drawn and ready. Hayden looked at Elle, who was too much in the line of fire for his liking.

"Chantiatus," Hayden uttered, with two fingers pointed at Elle. A protective forcefield surrounded her just before shots rang out from the officers on the roof. Hayden raised his left arm toward them as they fired. He could see several rounds hitting the forcefield around Elle, which enraged him.

Moments later, the officers in front of the building took the opportunity to act while Hayden was distracted. They fired off another barrage of rounds in unison. Hayden instinctively extended his right arm toward that front of the battle. Again, every round fired fell to the ground.

"Enough!" Hayden yelled, now attempting to hold back the rage from seeing that Elle was in mortal danger.

Hayden flicked his wrist on his left hand, and a forceful gust of wind knocked the officers on the roof back until they toppled off the other side. Hayden then dropped to a knee and pressed his right hand against the bullet-strewn grass. A strong tremor reverberated through the ground toward the multitude of officers in front of him, causing them to fall to the ground.

Hayden then raised his right hand to the sky, and as he did so, every police vehicle rose from the ground. Every firearm was snatched from the hands and belts of each officer and rose into the sky as well. As Hayden continued to raise his arm, the massive collection of vehicles and firearms ascended approximately a hundred feet off the ground. Every single person within visible range froze in place, eyes opened wide at the spectacle. Hayden's left hand now pointed toward the grouping of metal and plastic filling the sky.

Elle recognized the symbols of Darkness, Lightning, and Fire, all illuminating the back of Hayden's left hand at once. The amulet glimmered with brilliant intensity. A stream of power flowed from Hayden's hand, resembling a mixture of the powers from the symbols that Elle had just seen.

The outpouring of power collided with the objects in the sky. The cloud of debris swirled in darkness and began to implode inward, violently crackling with lightning and spouts of flame. The cluster continued to become smaller until Hayden dropped his hands to his sides. The conglomeration of objects fell from the sky, and the resultant sphere of dense metal hit the pavement in front of the police barricade, cracking the concrete around it and glowing red with heat. As everyone stumbled back up to their feet, they stood motionless, dumbfounded, and speechless.

"Hayden, surrender, please," the lead officer called out, this time without the bullhorn.

Hayden walked closer to the officers. "I can see that this isn't going to end, is it?"

"We can't just let you go," the officer replied.

"Yeah, that's what I thought," Hayden responded as he raised his right hand.

"Hayden!" Elle called out from behind him. He knew that she was asking him to temper his anger.

Hayden looked back at Elle and gave her a reassuring look. He grasped the amulet in his right hand, and the orange glow glistened brightly through his fingers.

In an instant, portals opened beneath every police officer on the scene, and they fell into them, instantaneously landing on the deck of a cruise ship that was in port in Long Beach, California. Hayden released the amulet, and the portals disappeared.

The news reporters and camera operators, still present, struggled to find words and simply continued to broadcast the events sans commentary. Hayden walked back to Elle, and as he approached her, he waved his right hand, and the forcefield around her dissipated.

"I'm going to end this nonsense now... peacefully,"

Hayden told Elle. "But I can't have you awake for this, darling. So trust me."

Elle nodded in acceptance. "Alright."

Hayden placed two fingers on Elle's forehead and sent her into the dreamscape. He caught her body as she fell and gently placed her on the grass. He then walked out to the barricade where the news media was attempting to explain what had happened to their viewers at home.

"Hayden, did you just kill that girl?" one of the reporters asked as he approached them.

"What the fuck?" Hayden responded indignantly. "No, I didn't kill her, you fool. I love her… she's asleep."

"You love her?" another reporter chimed in. "But you kidnapped her. Are the charges against you true? Where are all of those police officers?"

"Stop asking me useless questions," Hayden offered as a response. "We're going to rectify this situation right now. Are these newscasts national or what?"

A reporter finally spoke up. "National? No, by now, they're probably global."

"Perfect," Hayden said as he walked closer. "Don't worry, I'm not going to hurt you."

Hayden raised his left hand toward the crowd of reporters and clutched the amulet in his other hand. A brief surge of electricity shot from Hayden's right palm and bounced around from camera to camera, aligning all of their feeds into one. Hayden touched the camera of the reporter closest to him, sending a wave of energy up toward the sky. As a result, every television set across the world flicked on and set itself to the live feed.

"Prophesch'naya Con'di Illuminus Ane'dresaco," Hayden chanted, still clutching the amulet. He touched two of his fingers to his temple and pushed a series of thoughts into every mind across the globe.

Hayden let go of the amulet and lowered his other hand from the camera. The reporters and camera operators all looked at each other, confused as to why they were there. Hayden walked back through the grass toward Elle as the crowd of news media piled back into their respective vans and drove away.

Hayden knelt down and touched Elle's forehead. She instantly opened her eyes and gasped for air. After a moment of realization, she snapped back to reality.

"That was the most peaceful place I've ever been, Hayden," Elle said. "That's definitely not the dreamscape that I remember."

Hayden chuckled. "Well, the dreamscape is whatever I want it to be. When you and I have been inside before, it was always for a specific need, so I didn't spruce it up at all. However, I can make it a good place or a bad place, depending on what I need. Just now, I chose that particular iteration for you because I knew you'd like it."

Elle simply smiled back at him. She then sat up and noticed that the street was empty except for some wooden police barricades that still stood.

"Everyone is gone," Elle said in amazement.

"Yeah, everyone is gone. No one was hurt," Hayden replied. "No one is going to bother us about this again."

"Wait… how?" Elle inquired.

"I pushed a thought into the minds of everyone worldwide," Hayden responded. "No one thinks you're missing now, no one cares if we're together, and everyone has forgotten just about everything that has happened today."

"Oh… wow," Elle said, stunned at the ability of Hayden to exert his powers on such a grand scale. "Good!"

Elle stood and walked toward the front door of the apartment with Hayden. Before they entered, Hayden looked back at the street, still littered with wooden barricades and the lawn riddled with ammunition. He waved his left hand out in front of him, and any remaining remnants of the earlier activities turned to dust and floated away on the breeze.

They entered the apartment, and Hayden locked the

door behind them. He noted the time on the clock in the living room, 1:00 p.m.

"Are you ready for a shower?" Elle asked him.

"Yeah, after this morning, I'm definitely ready for a shower," Hayden replied.

Hayden walked into the master bathroom and looked back to find that Elle had followed him in. As he turned on the shower, he remarked. "Oh, are we showering together now?"

Elle responded by removing her clothes and stepping past Hayden into the steaming water, smiling at him as she passed.

❧ ❧ ❧ ❧ ❧ ❧

2:00 p.m., Armond's clock read. Everyone was already inside the house when Hayden and Elle appeared in the front yard. Armond urged everyone to remain inside while he went out to meet them.

As Armond approached Hayden and Elle on the front lawn, Hayden waved at him.

"Hayden," Armond said as he came closer. "I know what you did…"

"What I did?" Hayden replied inquisitively while

feigning ignorance.

"I was watching the television broadcast. Once I saw you put Elle in the dreamscape, I linked to you telepathically. Your thought push didn't affect me like everyone else in the world because of that."

"Okay, so what," Hayden said, laughing. "I did what I had to do, and no one got hurt."

"I agree with you, Hayden," Armond replied. "Just... sometimes, do you ever think that your power has grown too much?"

"No," Hayden responded flatly. "I've mastered that damn amulet."

"I could tell, Hayden," Armond continued. "You made up an entirely new spell from a combination of your powers. That hasn't been done since the time of Abbas. Not to mention being able to push a thought across the entire world. The most powerful users in the past were lucky to push a thought to even a dozen people at a time."

Hayden threw up his hands as if to convey a thought of whimsical delight in his abilities.

Armond sighed and turned back toward the house. "Everyone is inside already. Let's get this started."

Elle and Hayden followed Armond into the house, where Dan, Shaun, Lora, and Abby were seated in the living room. The television was on, but instead of any news of the day's events, a story about a local school book fair was being broadcast.

Hayden and Elle sat down next to each other on the couch across from everyone. Armond pulled up a chair from the dining room and joined them.

"As we all know very well," Armond started the meeting. "We've enjoyed four months of relative peace and quiet. However, I fear that with the arrival of Hayden and Elle back to this point in time, that false peace may soon be shattered. It is inevitable that Kali will come back at any time now."

"What do we do?" asked Dan.

"We wait… we prepare," Armond replied.

Hayden jumped in. "I have no doubt in my mind that Kali sensed me here on Earth today," he informed the group but purposely left out the details of the worldwide pulse of pushed thoughts as the reason she would have felt his presence. "She will be coming soon."

"Be ready to fight at a moment's notice," Armond told Hayden, Shaun, and Lora. "Dan and Abby, thank you for your support through all of this."

"Yeah, of course, no problem," Abby responded. Dan nodded his head in agreement with her.

"Kali has grown in power by a lot," Hayden added. "I don't know if Armond filled everyone in already, but she was able to transport Elle and myself off the planet to another galaxy. She trapped us near a black hole that dilated time for us so that a couple hours for us was four years here on Earth. When we finally got free, the planet was desolate… it was basically luck that we figured out a way to get back here to the present."

"Holy shit," exclaimed Abby. "So you guys basically time traveled?"

"Yes, a very rudimentary form of it," Hayden replied. "The process of traveling back four years in time was not instantaneous like you see in the movies. It was a journey that took us two years to complete."

"Wait…" Abby said, calculating the math in her head for a moment. "So you guys are actually twenty-four and eighteen, not twenty-two and sixteen? Even though you still look the same."

"Yeah, exactly," Hayden told her. "I had to use a spell to put our physical bodies in a state of suspended animation. Our physical bodies were functioning at the cellular level at the absolute lowest threshold to remain alive. That allowed us to survive the amount of time it took to get back. However, our minds were awake, functioning, communicating, and experiencing the effects of time the entire way back. To Elle and I, it feels like we should be in the year 2025, not 2023."

That's crazy," Abby replied. "So technically, Elle missed a bunch of important birthdays? That sucks!"

Dan chuckled and couldn't resist making a joke. "Abby always focusing on the top priorities, eh?"

"Shut up, Dan," Abby said. "Don't worry, Elle. When this is all over, we'll throw you a party big enough to make up for all of them."

"Thanks, Abby!" Elle replied with a smile.

Armond got the conversation back on track. "One point of encouragement is that while Kali may have grown in power, so has Hayden. After his last encounter with Kali, both the amulet and Hayden's latent abilities seem to have become exponentially stronger. I have personally witnessed him perform feats that I would have never thought possible."

"Well, that is actually encouraging," Lora replied.

"Lora and I have been working together to improve our abilities," Shaun added. "Though I still think that it would be a lot easier for us to do if we could borrow that amulet."

Hayden immediately responded. "Shaun, I've told you that the amulet is far too powerful and unpredictable to risk that. Even when it was still just a shard of stone, the thing almost corrupted me."

Shaun huffed in annoyance. "Oh, and you don't think we're strong enough to overcome that? How would we know if you never give us the chance? You're not perfect, Hayden."

Hayden looked toward Armond for some backup on the issue.

Armond readily obliged. "I have to agree with Hayden on this matter. Once he fashioned the shard into its new form, it became incredibly more potent… and since then, it's grown several times stronger than before. Besides, only the cognizant one was ever meant to wield more than one power at once. Also, the fact that two of the seven spells are etched into the amulet would come with an enormous risk if you were to attempt to use it. Neither of you possess the power to cast the spells."

"But again, we wouldn't know that for sure unless we tried," Shaun countered. Lora sat silently, not wanting to get involved.

"We also don't know that it wouldn't instantly kill you…" Dan said, entering the argument. "Is that a chance you want to take on a what-if?"

Shaun rebuked him. "Does your opinion matter here, Dan? You have no powers."

Hayden began to stand from his seat, now visibly

angered at Shaun's insolence toward his friend.

Armond quickly jumped in. "The answer is no, Shaun. Dan may not have powers, but he and Abby have been important members of this team, offering support and even putting their own lives in danger."

"Is this meeting over?" Shaun asked as he stood.

"It is," Armond replied. "Everyone go and get your mind in the right place. Be ready at a moment's notice."

Shaun walked toward the front door, turning back and motioning to Lora. "C'mon, I'm your ride. Let's go."

Lora stood and looked at the others with a sense of embarrassment on her face. She waved as she walked to the door to join Shaun.

After the two had exited the house, Abby finally commented what she had been holding back. "So Shaun is being sort of a douche."

Elle chimed in. "I feel bad for Lora. You can tell she doesn't care about the amulet like he does, but Shaun just tries to speak for her."

"You're right, Elle," Armond added. "I'll have a conversation with Shaun later and try to convince him to see reason. As for the rest of you, get some rest and prepare yourselves mentally for what is coming. Kali could be planning anything, and unfortunately, we won't know what until she's here."

As everyone stood, Dan asked the group. "Are you guys all down for some dinner at the Mexican restaurant?"

Hayden, Elle, and Abby all nodded their heads in agreement with Dan's suggestion.

"I'd love a nice relaxing night out after all this," Hayden replied.

Armond responded. "You all have a good time… I need to call my brother and catch up."

Dan, Hayden, Elle, and Abby gathered their belongings and made their way out to the driveway.

"Hey Dan, do you mind if Elle and I ride with you and Abby?" Hayden asked as the group neared his car.

"What, you get tired of flying around?" Dan said as he laughed.

"I just want to relax and be normal for one night," Hayden responded.

"Touché," Dan conceded.

Elle and Hayden climbed into the back seat of Dan's car while Abby took the passenger seat. The group then began the ten-minute drive to Eduardo Quesada's Mexican Restaurant.

Two minutes into the drive, Abby turned down the stereo and posed a question. "Do you guys think that Shaun would ever try to take the amulet?"

"Like steal it from Hayden?" Dan replied with a question.

"Yeah," Abby followed up. "Like, do you think he'd take it that far?"

"He better not!" Elle replied. "Besides, he'd be insane if he ever thought he could physically take it from Hayden."

Dan joked. "Oh, damn, Elle is sticking up for her man."

Elle laughed in response to Dan's jest. "I'm just saying… this is the first time I've met him, but he seems like an ass."

"You're not wrong, sister," Abby replied. "It's not the first time he's brought it up… and you're right, Elle, he would stand no chance against Hayden."

"You guys are gonna make me blush," Hayden joked.

"Oh, now there's some comedy," Dan said as he pulled into a parking spot at the restaurant.

As the group entered the restaurant, Abby walked up and touched a photograph that the owner had hung in the waiting area of Paige with the caption "rest in peace" printed below.

"We miss you, girl," Abby said as she put her fingers on the picture frame. Hayden and Dan looked at each other with expressions of somber remembrance.

As the group walked back into the dining area to their usual booth, Elle remarked. "I wish I could've met Paige. I can tell you guys all really cared about her."

Hayden smiled at Elle's kind words. Abby turned to Elle and replied. "Yeah, she was pretty great… I'm sure she would've liked you, Elle."

"…Unlike her sister," Dan joked before he realized how stupid the words coming out of his mouth were. Abby immediately scolded him with a look of disgust.

"The fuck, dude?" Hayden responded. "You're buying the first three rounds of drinks for that dumbass comment."

Elle's expression changed to a look of embarrassment and dejection. Dan immediately tried to remedy the situation. "Elle, I'm sorry… sometimes I say shit I don't mean before I even think. You're the greatest addition to our group since Abby." He was obviously trying to appease Abby's displeasure with him at the same time.

"I mean, I've had this thought in the back of my mind," Elle replied to the group as a whole. "What if, like, Hayden is able to somehow save Kali?"

Elle then directed the next part of the question to Hayden, "I know you and her were in a relationship before all this happened. So if she went back to normal… I've been asking myself, then what happens to you and me?"

Abby gave Hayden a wide-eyed and concerned look that seemed to say, without words. "She's genuinely insecure about this. You need to reassure her."

Dan commented. "Dude, do you guys need a minute alone to talk? Abby and I can go sit at the bar."

"No, you guys are fine," Hayden replied and then spoke to Elle. "I love you. Nothing is going to change that. There is no person, no event, no circumstance that is ever going to cause you and I to not be together. No one comes before you, Elle. I promise you that. Kali is in my past, and no matter what happens, that's not going to change. My present and my future belong to you alone."

Tears ran down Elle's cheeks as she firmly hugged Hayden. Abby took the opportunity to suggest that she and Elle go to the restroom together to give Elle a chance to freshen up.

After Elle and Abby walked away toward the restroom, Dan guiltily told Hayden. "Dude, I'm sorry… that was stupid of me."

"Not going to disagree with you there," Hayden replied. "But honestly, I didn't know that Elle had such a deep insecurity about that… so if any good came of your comment, it's that we got to talk about it."

"True," Dan said hesitantly. "I hope she doesn't think I'm a complete asshole now though."

Hayden grabbed Dan's shoulder and joked. "Think? We've all known that for some time."

"Funny…" Dan replied, accepting the humorous jab as a consequence of his actions.

As the two finished their conversation, the waiter came by the table. Hayden and Dan put in drink orders for everyone.

In the restroom, Elle rinsed her face with cold water and patted it dry with a paper towel before touching up her foundation and blush.

Abby stood behind her and offered words of reassurance. "He does really love you, Elle. I've known Hayden a long time. I can see how he feels by the way he looks at you and the way he acts."

Elle smiled at Abby in the mirror. "Thank you. You've been such a good friend to me. I know I'm new to the group, and everyone has been so open and accepting."

"Girl, you are amazing!" Abby replied. "I'm so glad I came into our group… and to be honest, you're the best thing to ever happen to Hayden."

"Thank you," Elle said as she finished up her makeup.

Abby and Elle returned to the booth to join Hayden

and Dan just as the drinks were dropped off by the waiter. The group ordered their dinner and spent the remainder of the meal focusing on happier topics.

After dinner concluded, the group walked back out to the parking lot. "You guys want a ride home?" Dan asked Hayden and Elle.

"Naw, that's alright, bro…" Hayden told him. "Get Abby home. Elle and I will travel by air."

The group said their goodbyes, and Dan and Abby departed. Elle grabbed hold of Hayden, and the two made the short flight back to their apartment.

"Sorry for kind of breaking down back there," Elle told Hayden as they walked into the living room and down the hallway.

"Don't be sorry," Hayden replied. "If you ever have questions, doubts, or troubling thoughts like that, just promise that you'll talk to me."

Elle shook her head in agreement. "I promise."

As they readied themselves for bed, Elle interrupted Hayden as he was beginning to change into his pajamas. She placed her hand on his chest as a motion that he should stop. Elle gently pushed Hayden back onto the bed and then removed her clothes before joining him. Following Elle's completely unambiguous cues, Hayden acquiesced to her lead, and they made love before ending the night with some well-deserved sleep.

Chapter Eight

End of Days

Twenty-seven days passed uneventfully, each one putting Armond more and more on edge. Hayden, Elle, Dan, and Abby seized the lack of Kali's return to enjoy the peace and quiet. They went out for nightly dinners and daytime trips to the beach, theme parks, sporting events, and a handful of group shopping trips. In mid-July, Abby took Elle out on a girl's day to get their nails done and then bonded over a trip to Joey's Frozen Yogurt in downtown Anaheim.

The next morning, July 21st, the group decided to take an impromptu trip to Chino Hills State Park for some local hiking. Dan and Abby arrived at Hayden and Elle's apartment at 7:00 a.m., and the group began to pack the trunk of his car with bottled water and snacks.

As Hayden brought out the last of the group's preparations, a striking chill swept through the air. Elle looked over at Hayden with concern written on her face. Hayden quickened his pace and joined the others near the car.

"This can't be good," Dan said.

A dark, swirling cloud formed in the sky above the neighborhood. Hayden instinctively moved in front of Elle to protect her from harm.

"Dan, Abby," Hayden spoke in a raised voice above the wind. "Take Elle inside with you and keep her safe."

They didn't have time to respond to Hayden's request. Lightning cut through the sky and struck the pavement thirty feet in front of the group before they had a chance to move. As their eyes adjusted back from the overload of light, they saw Kali standing on the now-smoking pavement.

"Shit!" Abby exclaimed, now frozen in fear.

Hayden's amulet began to glow a steady orange as Kali walked toward the group. Elle, still in back of Hayden, put her arms tightly around him, fearing for her life. Kali walked straight up the driveway to Hayden, stopping less than a foot from where he was standing. She looked at Dan and Abby momentarily.

"Hayden…" Kali started, now turning her gaze back to him. "I'm sorry for what I did to you and the girl. Can you forgive me?"

Dan and Abby exchanged confused looks. Hayden couldn't find words to reply to her.

Kali continued. "You, of all people, know what the power of the Alva'ci can do to a person... how it can corrupt even the most noble of people. I've made mistakes, but I wasn't myself. I just want your forgiveness, and I want to be with you again."

Hayden felt Elle tremble as Kali finished her request. He placed his hand on Elle's arm to calm and reassure her.

Kali took a few steps to the side so that she could see Elle. Hayden quickly repositioned himself to block her.

"Hayden," Kali pressed on. "I'll even let the girl go. She can go live in peace. Just have Dan and Abby take her away from here, and then you and I can be together again... like it was meant to be. Like you wanted before the Alva'ci stole me from you. I know you want that again."

"I can't do that, Kali," Hayden finally replied. "I won't do that... but I will try to help you if you let me."

Kali tried to hide the change in demeanor on her face. "You mean you love her? You'd choose her over me? After all the time we've known each other. After you anguished for years to have me come back and be with you?"

Dan let out an audible groan as he felt the

conversation taking a turn for the worse. Abby moved to the other side of the car, closer to Dan.

Hayden finally revealed what he had felt for months now. "Kali, you're trying to appeal to my sympathy and relate to my experience overcoming the corruption of the shard… like it's something that I can help you overcome also. I saw the effect that the Alva'ci's power already had on you. You aren't struggling with corruption. It's already taken you over. You're not fooling me, Kali… and yes, I do love Elle. You and I had our time, but it is long over."

"You're a fool, Hayden," Kali menacingly retorted. "You and I can rule the world together with the power we have. We can rule the universe."

"No," Hayden stated simply.

Kali's expression turned to pure hatred. She turned to face the fruit tree that stood on the front lawn and stretched her left arm out in its direction. Hayden and the others watched as every apple hanging from the branches withered and fell, turning to dust as they hit the grass below.

"Time, Hayden…" Kali said. "I will erase this insignificant girl that you love so much from time. Then, after you watch her vanish from existence, I will kill you. I will take your powers, and I will destroy every last thing on this planet."

Elle was now continuously shaking with fear, unable to keep herself from sobbing out loud.

"Look at how pathetic she is, Hayden," Kali berated. "She is nothing! She isn't worthy of you… isn't worthy of your love. Move aside, and let me send her to join the rest of her family in hell."

Hayden had, until now, largely kept his composure. However, Kali's latest round of insolence ignited his temper. Elle could feel a deep chill emanate from Hayden's body, like an arctic wind that cuts through every layer of clothing, as both of his hands suddenly came ablaze with symbols of power.

As Hayden swept his right arm out to his side, three portals appeared near Dan's car. Armond, Lora, and Shaun fell through the portals and quickly realized what was occurring.

"Elle is more worthy of my love than you ever were," Hayden's words rolled off his tongue, sharp as a knife.

Dan pulled Abby down to the ground behind his car to take cover. Armond quickly joined them and tried to get Elle's attention to get her to safety. Elle hesitated momentarily, but as Shaun and Lora moved closer to Kali, she took the opportunity to run to Armond, Dan, and Abby.

Shaun raised both of his hands and pointed them toward Kali. A torrent of water flowed from his right hand, and a stream of ice from his left. Kali effortlessly deflected both.

Hayden turned to make sure that Elle had gotten to safety with the others when Kali seized the opportunity to land a blow. She raised both hands toward Hayden and struck him with a duet of lightning bolts.

Hayden was thrown to the ground from the blast and stunned. As he fell, the amulet came loose from his neck and landed several feet away on the driveway. Shaun walked over to where the amulet lay and knelt down.

Armond yelled out with urgency. "Shaun, don't do it!"

Shaun disregarded Armond's plea and grasped the amulet in his right hand. The resulting look of enveloping pain on his face was instantaneous. Shaun attempted to drop the amulet, but his effort was futile. Everyone but Kali watched in horror as Shaun's body began to intensely glow with an orange hue. Within moments, he turned to ash.

"What a pompous fool," Kali remarked after watching Shaun's demise. "He actually thought he could wield that power."

Hayden began to slowly recover from Kali's offensive. Meanwhile, Lora reached her hand down to the soil and sent a shockwave through the ground toward Kali.

Kali immediately touched her own hand against

the driveway and absorbed the attempted attack. She then touched her other hand to the ground. A multitude of roots sprung up around Lora and wrapped themselves around her body, immobilizing her. Kali approached Lora and placed her hand on Lora's forehead.

"Another step closer to finishing what my sister started," Kali said as she forced an overwhelming electrical current through Lora's body until she was nothing but a charred corpse on the lawn.

"Holy shit!" Dan said in a panic. "Hayden, get up, buddy!"

Kali walked toward the amulet as Hayden was beginning to work his way up to his hands and knees, still reeling from the blow Kali had landed.

Kali stepped over the amulet and walked toward the back of the car, where Armond, Dan, Abby, and Elle were taking cover. Hayden had finally risen to his feet when Kali grabbed Elle by the neck, dragging her out into the open.

"Kali, let her go!" yelled Hayden. "This is between you and me."

"You're right, Hayden," Kali responded. "It is between me and you… and I'm going to strike you right in the heart."

As Kali let go of Elle's neck, she raised her left hand toward her. A blast of energy hit Elle and knocked her to the ground. Hayden swept up the amulet and placed it back around his neck as he ran to Elle's side. She didn't appear to be injured.

"What did you do?" demanded Hayden.

Kali took several steps back and grinned, mockingly telling Hayden. "Exactly what I said I was going to do… your precious little bitch is now going backward in time until she ceases to exist."

"I won't let that happen!" Hayden screamed.

"Don't worry, Hayden," Kali replied with a malicious grin still painting her face. "I won't kill you yet. Oh, and look on the bright side, dear… it will be a relatively painless death for both her and your child."

Hayden was visibly shaken. "What?" was all he could manage to utter, with shock and disbelief setting in.

Hayden placed his hand on Elle's pelvis and closed his eyes in concentration. He sensed what Kali was cruelly taunting him with. Elle was about four weeks pregnant. When Elle read the fear on Hayden's face, she began to cry.

Hayden's fear quickly turned to anger and determination. He rebuked Kali's underestimation of his power. "I'll just reverse whatever you've done, Kali."

Hayden placed his hands on Elle's forehead and chest, closed his eyes, and concentrated on negating whatever magic Kali had used on her.

"You can't do it, can you, Hayden?" Kali said smugly. "Why do you think I've been gone for so long? I've been perfecting my powers over time. Soon, I'll be more powerful than you could ever imagine."

As Hayden reached up for the amulet, Kali grabbed him by the neck with one hand. With the other hand, she summoned the roots that had bound Lora and used them to hold Hayden's hands at his sides.

"No, you don't..." Kali said through an evil laugh. "Besides, that amulet won't help you save her."

Hayden struggled against the roots, and the symbol of fire lit on the back of both his hands. Before he had a chance to take any action, Kali interrupted. "Let's go somewhere fun," she said as she opened a portal. Hayden and Kali vanished.

Armond, Abby, and Dan ran over to Elle and helped her to her feet.

"What do we do?" Abby asked.

المبهر

Chapter Nine

The Forbidden Spell

Hayden's portal opened, and he arrived back on Earth in the middle of Craig Regional Park, near his apartment. Armond was leading Elle, Dan, and Abby through the park as a shortcut to get to his house after they discovered Dan's car no longer worked.

As Hayden walked toward the group, Armond ran up to meet him. "Are you okay? Did you defeat Kali?" he asked.

"I'm fine," Hayden responded. "And no, Kali is still out there. We fought. She's gotten insanely powerful, but I managed to injure her. That's when she made another comment about Elle. I had to use the opportunity to come back. How is she?"

"Come and see for yourself," Armond urged Hayden as they walked closer to the group. "Kali wasn't lying… Elle has regressed, by my best guess, to about eleven years of age. You've been gone an hour. At this rate, she'll be gone in two hours and twelve minutes."

As they approached the group, Hayden could immediately see the reversal of maturation in Elle's body. He rushed up to comfort her.

"What do we do, Hayden?" Dan asked. "Is there any way to stop this?"

Hayden stood silently next to Elle in the wide-open field. The expanse of grass and trees that surrounded the group would have been picturesque at any other point in time. Hayden and Elle stared into each other's eyes with a mutual feeling of hopelessness.

Elle reached out and grabbed Hayden's hand. Her touch had always brought him joy and a sense of peace... but now he could feel the trembling fear resonating from her body into his, with her hand as the conduit.

Hayden had an overwhelming feeling that there must be some power he held that would save Elle, but he didn't know what. He put his hand on Elle's chest and grasped the amulet, which blazed with the intensity of a star. An aura of gold surrounded Elle as Hayden tapped the depths of his power.

Nothing. In a fit of despondent rage at his inability to

save Elle, lightning crackled through the clear sky and split a nearby tree in half. Abby jumped back in shock at the sight. Hayden turned back to Elle and simply held her in his arms, his mind still fervently searching for an answer.

After several minutes of silence, Hayden started pacing back and forth in thought. His instincts clashed in his mind with everything he had previously been told. No one had survived what he was now contemplating, according to Armond. However, Hayden also thought about the fact that no one before him was ever imbued with this much power. He had, after all, fused his powers before to create an entirely new spell. The thought gave him hope… or was it simply vanity bouncing around in his mind?

Regardless, Hayden had reached a decision. He would rather die trying to keep Elle safe than give up and watch her and their child cease to exist… and he knew that he had to be sure that she would still be okay when he left to go face Kali again. He had no clue if he would be able to return again before Armond's time estimate was up.

Hayden turned to Elle, looked into her eyes, and took both her hands into his. In place of his previously somber expression, a new look of determination filled his face.

Without even needing a telepathic connection, Armond immediately sensed what Hayden had been contemplating.

"Don't do it," Armond begged Hayden, with a grave look splayed across his face. "It is a desperate resort and has always ended in tragedy."

Hayden glanced at Armond. "It's the only thing to be done now," he replied matter-of-factly.

Armond stared off into the distance with a now despondent gaze. He was certain that the world was about to lose its only hope of survival. Hayden was embarking on a course that would kill both him and Elle. Armond had studied the history and lore long enough and had no doubt in his mind as to the outcome of Hayden's newly concocted plan. Dan and Abby were unsure what Armond and Hayden were arguing about, but the worried looks they gave each other indicated that they understood the grave repercussions.

"Hayden, you should listen to Armond," Abby said, her voice shaking. "We can figure something out together."

Hayden didn't respond. He turned back to face Elle and stared into her eyes as if to possibly say goodbye. Hayden kissed Elle on the forehead and then squeezed her hands as a hopeful gesture before he uttered his next words:

"E'it ad'a layadänte."

Elle felt each and every syllable of the spell reverberate in her bones as Hayden spoke them. An indescribably stark chill coursed through her veins, and she instinctively pulled Hayden in close to her for protection from whatever the feeling was taking over her body. Moments after they embraced, Armond noticed a faint white aura surrounding the two before they collapsed on the ground.

Armond, fearing the worst, rushed over to Hayden and Elle. He was positive that Hayden's lack of obedience to his warnings about casting the forbidden spell had resulted in both his and Elle's death. This was, after all, the precedent of several thousand years when others had attempted to use this spell. Armond placed his hands on the faces of Elle and Hayden. They were cold to the touch, freezing cold, to be exact.

Armond gazed hopelessly off into the distance as the world seemed to crumble around him to its eventual demise. He was about to rise to his feet when he noticed an unfamiliar marking on Hayden's left tricep, right above his elbow. He had never seen this mark before in any of the ancient texts. He thought for a moment and then reached over and checked Elle's arm.

"She has the same mark…" he mused to himself.

Dan frantically asked Armond. "Are they dead?"

Moments later, Hayden suddenly awoke, gasping in a deep breath. He was immediately followed by Elle reacting in the same manner. Armond fell back in shock and sat in the grass, as Hayden and Elle looked into each other's eyes. Elle managed to get herself up to her hands and knees. She crawled over to Hayden and sought the comfort of his embrace.

"This… this is unprecedented," Armond stated.

Hayden rose from the ground and helped Elle to her feet as well. Armond pointed out the markings on their arms, and Hayden inspected Elle's, running his fingers over it. He had never seen the symbol before, but he assumed that it had something to do with the forbidden spell.

Hayden placed his hand back on Elle's chest and closed his eyes, focusing on her body's cellular activity.

"She has stopped de-aging!" Hayden proclaimed.

"It worked!" Abby screamed in joy. "I'm sorry I doubted you Hayden."

Dan's excitement was also tempered with slight confusion. "If it worked, though, then why does she still look like she's eleven?"

"Hayden stopped the effect," Armond replied. "I'm not sure if he can reverse what has already been done."

Elle felt a mixture of both relief and fear at the same time.

"Please don't tell me I'm stuck like this!" she exclaimed,

looking around at everyone in the group for a possible answer.

"We'll do some research and find an answer, Elle," Armond tried to say reassuringly.

"I know the answer," Hayden said. "I'm going to have to leave again."

Elle sighed and told him. "Be safe, I need you."

"I'll be safe, Elle," Hayden replied. "But if I don't come back…"

"Don't say that!" Elle interrupted.

"If I don't come back," Hayden continued, giving her a look of genuine concern. "I want you to be happy… I want you to raise that baby to be a person who is just as amazing as you are."

Hayden then spoke to the entire group. "…and I want all of you to promise me that you'll look out for Elle."

Dan nodded his head, with tears welling in his eyes. "You got it, buddy… we promise." Abby, who was already crying, hugged Dan.

Armond touched Hayden's shoulder and told him. "I have faith in you. This story does not end here."

"Thank you, Armond," Hayden said.

"I still don't understand, though," Armond continued. "What exactly did the forbidden spell do other than stop the de-aging effect."

"No?" replied Hayden. "The Abassilon Prophecy. 'We shall share this path...' is a very rough translation of the forbidden spell. More accurately, it would be, 'the two will be like one, their essence inseparable.'"

"Interesting," Armond said. "But other than alluding to the spell, what significance does the Prophecy have?"

Hayden stepped back several feet from Elle. "Trust me," he told her as he raised his right hand in her direction. Her eyes widened, and Armond lunged forward toward Elle in instinctual panic as Hayden released a stream of lightning at her. The electrical current stopped short of hitting her and instead circulated around Hayden's body until it dissipated.

Armond stood in place with his mouth agape. Dan finally broke the silence. "What?! Elle is immune?"

Hayden's face became serious again. "It's time to go and finish this."

Hayden gave Elle one last look. "I love you," he told her right before vanishing into a portal.

ை ை ை ை ை ை

Hayden arrived back, exiting the portal just outside the orbit of Mars. The amulet was glowing bright orange around his neck. He could see Kali in the distance, injured but expediently nursing herself back to full strength.

As Hayden cautiously approached Kali, she placed her hand over her wounded side, and a faint purple light radiated from it.

"That lucky shot won't happen again," she told Hayden. "It's time for me to take your powers and rule this universe."

Kali's subsequent attack was brutally savage. She fired off a salvo of energy bursts while simultaneously hurling fragments of asteroid at Hayden from all directions. While he blocked and deflected the majority of Kali's attacks, several managed to land. However, Kali was infuriated to discover that her successes had not significantly injured her adversary.

"Tell me how to reverse what you did to Elle," Hayden demanded.

"I'll never tell you how to save that insufferable little whore," Kali refused. "You really cried and moaned for so long about you and I getting back together. Then all of a sudden, she comes along, and you impregnate her. Do you want to know what I want? I wish that I had taken the time to slowly torture her in front of you. That you could hear her screams of agony and watch as I separated her limbs from her body. Then, just for you, right before I killed her I'd shove a blade into her belly. Before I moved on to your demise, I would let you watch the life fade from her eyes while she tried to apologize to you through gurgling blood-filled gasps for air… to tell you that she's sorry for being a feeble, worthless waste of flesh."

"You are sick in the head, Kali," Hayden replied. "Let's get this charade over with."

"Gladly," Kali responded and began another round of attacks.

Hayden anticipated the pattern of Kali's incoming barrage and easily deflected it, sending blasts of energy into unsuspecting space debris that disintegrated on impact. The battle continued to rage back and forth. Hayden ramped up the power of his attacks, still attempting to incapacitate Kali without killing her.

Finally, tapping into the extra depths of power that the Alva'ci had unlocked for him in the dreamscape, Hayden launched a dazzling offensive. An array of brilliant light shone from the amulet, and it seemed as if the stars around them dimmed. An enormous column of energy hurtled toward Kali, eclipsing her ability to defend against it. With speeds more resembling teleportation than flight, Hayden appeared next to Kali, wielding a blade of light. Remorsefully, he thrust the instrument of destruction into her abdomen. As he withdrew the blade, Kali's blood poured from the wound.

"I'm sorry," he told her.

Kali placed her hand over the wound, attempting to stem the bleeding. She quickly found that no amount of pressure was going to remedy the injury. Blood covered her hand and soaked her clothing. Within a few seconds, the blood started to run down her thighs, and Kali knew definitively the gravity of her situation.

"We loved each other," Kali said to Hayden. "You said you wanted nothing more than to be with me. Yet, here you stand, killing me."

A dazzling orange light rose from Kali's body and rushed toward the amulet. The final remnants of power from the Alva'ci had been absorbed into the stone. Immediately after, a purple-tinted haze surrounded Kali. The energy shot forth from her body in a shockwave. The amulet drew in the majority of the energy blast, with a faint portion of it trailing off into space behind Kali.

"I'm sorry for everything I've done," Kali cried out to Hayden through increasingly labored breathing. The effects of corruption from the power of the Alva'ci were slowly beginning to fade.

"Palkischus Abradyschnavya Istatim," Hayden uttered. He compassionately held Kali. On the inside, his mind was raging at the cruelty of fate at the end of things.

Kali felt a chill take over her body as if ice had been

poured directly into her bloodstream. The pain began to ease just as she slipped into a state of suspended animation. The wound and her body were in stasis.

"Chantiatus," Hayden muttered, bringing up a forcefield around Kali. He wondered if he would live to regret his split decision to keep Kali alive. However, for all the pain and destruction she had caused under the corruption of her powers, he couldn't stand to watch her die.

Hayden opened a portal and carried Kali's still body through it. They arrived near the planet Moira as the other end of the portal flashed open. Hayden located a suitable place to store Kali's body where it would be safe from further harm. As he descended onto a nearby planet outside the severe gravitational field of the black hole, Hayden placed Kali in a small cave and sealed the entrance with large boulders.

"Kali," Hayden spoke into the expanse of the lifeless planet's surface as if he were speaking to her. "I am truly sorry that it had to come to this. You will be safe here until I can figure out what to do with you. Rest easy."

A bright flash illuminated the grey skies as Hayden opened a portal to Armond's home back on Earth.

مخيف

Chapter Ten

The Quickening of the Amulet

Hayden walked through the portal into Armond's living room. His posture testified to the weight of anguish that his mind bore. Dried blood stained his clothing and skin. Elle, Dan, Abby, and Armond were all sitting on the couch, anxiously awaiting his return. As he appeared in front of them, they sprung to their feet in unison.

"Damn, bro," Dan said solemnly as he observed both the copious amount of blood covering Hayden and the pained expression marring his face.

Hayden took the amulet from around his neck and dropped it on the coffee table.

"It is finished," he said simply in a monotone voice.

Elle ran to Hayden and embraced him. As he wrapped his arms around her, Hayden felt a resurgence of hope wash over him. After a few moments, Abby, Dan, and Armond walked over and joined the hug. Hayden finally took a seat on the couch next to Elle once the reunion had concluded.

"So, is Kali… dead?" Abby asked.

"I don't want to talk about it," Hayden informed her.

"Okay, that's understandable," Abby relented. "Just know that we're all here for you if you ever want to talk about what happened."

"I know," Hayden said. "It's all just too raw and bitter at the moment."

"Do you know how to reverse Elle's de-aging?" Armond asked.

"I don't know," Hayden admitted. "At the end of the battle, the amulet absorbed new powers. I haven't even tried to explore those yet. I will figure it out, though."

"Well, for now, please feel free to use my shower to clean up," Armond said. "I will grab you some clean clothes."

"Thank you," Hayden replied. "I could use that."

Hayden made his way into the bathroom, placing his blood-stained clothes into a plastic bag. As the hot water poured over him, the tension and pain in his body began to fade. Hayden watched as the water circling the drain slowly turned from a red-tinted reminder of his battle to clear. As he stood in the almost scalding stream of water, Hayden heard the door click open.

"Thank you for everything you've done for me," Elle said as she sat on the bathroom counter. "I love you."

"I love you too, Elle," Hayden replied over the sounds of the splashing water. "I promise that I'll get everything back to normal."

"I know you will. I have total faith in you," Elle said. "But the most important thing to me is that you're back and you're safe."

After Hayden's shower, the group spent a few hours hanging out. The mood in the room alternated between complete reflective silence and cautiously optimistic relief. Around 10:00 p.m., the group decided to retire to their respective homes and reconvene in the morning.

"You two need a ride home?" Abby asked Hayden and Elle.

"Honestly, I think I just want to walk," Hayden replied. "If that's okay with you, Elle?"

"Yeah, that would be a welcome change from flying around and using portals," Elle told him.

"I'll see you guys in the morning then," Abby said as she waved and got into her car.

Hayden and Elle walked through the neighborhood and into the park to cut across on the way back home.

"Are you okay?" Elle asked as she took Hayden's hand in her own.

"I will be," Hayden admitted. "Everything that you and I have been through recently is just a lot to process. We've both lost so many people, friends and family."

"We have," Elle replied. "It has been a painful couple of years, but we still have each other. I don't think I would have made it through all the hurt and loss if it weren't for you. You're my family now."

"We'll continue making it through every day together," Hayden added.

Once they arrived at the apartment, Hayden prepared a quick snack. As they sat next to each other on the couch, Elle began to drift off to sleep. Hayden carried her to the bedroom and tucked her under the blankets. He stood next to the bed for a few minutes and watched as she slept peacefully.

ᔕ ᔕ ᔕ ᔕ ᔕ ᔕ

Hayden awoke the next morning to the sweet aroma of maple syrup. He opened his eyes to see Elle in the kitchen, making pancakes.

"You didn't come to bed last night?" Elle asked when

she saw him finally stir.

"I'm sorry, I was up trying to figure out these new powers within the amulet," Hayden replied. "I must have eventually just passed out on the couch."

"Come eat," Elle said as she placed their plates on the dining room table.

After breakfast, they readied themselves for everyone to assemble at the apartment. Dan brought an assortment of donuts along for everyone to snack on. As they gathered in the front room, Hayden got right down to business.

"I'm ready to give this a shot," he advised.

Hayden held the amulet in his hand and concentrated. A bright purple light began to shimmer from the stone. After a few minutes with no obvious effects, Hayden focused harder and pulled more energy into his efforts. Wisps of orange light intertwined themselves with the hues of purple.

"Wow," Dan stated as he pointed to the clock on the wall. The second hand had slightly slowed its pace.

Thirty seconds later, Hayden fell to the floor in exhaustion. Elle helped him up and into a chair.

"I'm going to go into the dreamscape," Hayden declared. "There must be more to this, and that orb may have some answers."

"Be careful," Armond advised.

"I will. This might take a while, so I'm going to lie down in my bedroom. If you all want to hang out, I'm sure that Elle wouldn't mind the company."

"Of course we'll stay," Abby said. "Now that everything is peaceful, Elle and I can start planning that belated birthday party for her."

"I'm down to plan parties," Dan added.

As the day wore into night, Hayden had still not awakened from his trip into the dreamscape. At eleven o'clock, Elle assured the others that everything would be okay if they headed home and promised to call them if anything happened. Abby, Dan, and Armond reluctantly agreed and set off for their own homes.

Elle walked into the bedroom, where Hayden was still unconscious. As she watched his chest rise and fall with each breath, Elle silently admired Hayden's dedication to caring for her. She crawled into the bed and curled up next to Hayden.

❧ ❧ ❧ ❧ ❧ ❧

Hayden finally woke from the dreamscape the next morning, noting how tired he was despite being unconscious for almost twenty-four hours. Elle's arm was draped over his chest, and her cheek rested on his shoulder. She began to stir from Hayden's sudden movement as he came out of the dreamscape and back into reality.

"Good morning. Welcome back," she said, with a peaceful smile on her face. "You were in there for quite a while."

"Yeah, I can tell," Hayden replied. "I'm exhausted, but I learned a lot."

"So you can reverse this?"

"I think so," Hayden replied. "First, I have to go to Yosemite though. The cave Paige was killed in has a large slab of rock. Apparently, there are a number of spells inscribed on it. The Alva'ci, even when dormant underground for all those years, still continued to acquire knowledge. It recorded everything it could on that stone slab, including some of the secrets about this new power."

"There won't be any danger there?" Elle asked.

"No danger, just a quick trip there and back," Hayden assured her.

"Okay, I'll call Abby and have her come over after we shower and get ready to keep me company."

A couple hours later, Abby arrived at the apartment. Hayden opened a portal and vanished in search of answers.

ভ৯ ভ৯ ভ৯ ভ৯ ভ৯ ভ৯

Hayden stepped out of the portal into the darkness of the cave. The entrance that he had carried Paige's body out of the year before appeared to be sealed. He activated the power of Light and illuminated the cavern.

As he slid his hand over the smooth, dark slab, Hayden looked around the room and recalled the somber events that had transpired the last time he'd been there. Focusing back on the task at hand, Hayden removed the amulet from around his neck. As it began to glow in his hand, Hayden touched it to the top of the slab.

The etchings along the sides of the stone lit up. Moments later, an additional grouping of text began to shine on the top of the slab. Hayden held the amulet in his outstretched hand as it began to glimmer with hints of purple light. Like a rush of wind filling his soul, the eons of knowledge contained in the inscriptions filled his mind.

ভ৯ ভ৯ ভ৯ ভ৯ ভ৯ ভ৯

When Hayden arrived back at the apartment, Elle and Abby were curled up on the couch under a large plush blanket, quietly enjoying a movie. Elle reached for the remote on the coffee table to put the film on hold.

"Keep it going," Hayden insisted as he sat next to Elle on the couch. "Let's all just relax and finish the movie. We can talk after."

"Sounds good to me," Elle said as she placed the remote back on the table and cuddled up against Hayden.

Two hours later, Elle clicked off the television, and the girls shifted their attention to Hayden to hear his news.

"So the orb was telling the truth again," Hayden declared. "The Alva'ci recorded everything it learned over all those years into hidden writings, all contained in the cave in Yosemite. The spells related to Kali's powers over time were included, except for one that it apparently never figured out."

"So you can reverse this?" Elle asked, her delight and hopefulness evident in her mannerisms.

"I can," Hayden replied. "Once I cast the spell, it will work just like the one that Kali did. You will change back to exactly how you were over the course of an hour or so."

"Okay, let's do it!" Elle gleefully exclaimed.

Hayden stood in front of Elle and grasped the amulet, while Abby stood nearby and watched the unprecedented events unfold. Hayden pointed his palm at Elle and recited the words to a spell in his mind. The amulet began to glisten, and a swath of purple light flowed from

Hayden's palm, encircling Elle's body.

"Did it work?" Elle asked as the wisps of light faded away.

"I think so," Hayden replied. "We will know for sure as time goes by."

"So, what else did you learn in there?" Abby asked.

"There was the spell that I just did," Hayden said. "Also, the opposite one of that, which is what Kali cast. Then, a spell that should slow or freeze time, which I think was what I almost accomplished yesterday. The writing of the Alva'ci alluded to the existence of at least one more spell, but all it said in reference to it was 'TDOA.' I have no idea what that means, but I think it's related to a story the orb told me concerning a lady named Bilv'at."

"Well, do you guys want to make some popcorn and watch another movie while we wait?" Elle suggested.

"I'm down for that," Abby agreed.

Elle found a comedy film to watch. The three of them had all seen it before, but no one objected to watching it again. They were all too preoccupied with the effects of the spell manifesting to devote their full attention to the plot of a new movie.

About halfway through the movie, Elle reached over for the remote and hit pause. She ventured across the living room and switched on the light to reveal what she had already noticed.

"Your body is back to normal!" Abby exclaimed. "How do you feel?"

"I feel excellent," Elle replied as she looked herself over. "It actually worked!"

"Now, let's make sure that the baby is still okay," Hayden suggested.

"Yes, please do," Elle agreed as she sat on the couch and leaned back into the cushion.

Hayden placed his hand over Elle's pelvis, closed his eyes, and concentrated. Abby and Elle waited in silent suspense for a verdict.

"Everything is good," Hayden finally announced as he opened his eyes.

Elle breathed a sigh of relief, and Abby clasped her hands in a celebratory gesture.

"Tomorrow, I'll call and schedule a doctor's appointment," Elle said.

ಎ ಎ ಎ ಎ ಎ ಎ

FIVE DAYS LATER:

Hayden woke Elle up at eight o'clock in the morning. As she stirred, she noticed the sweet aromas radiating from the kitchen. Hayden was already showered, dressed, and noticeably chipper, considering the fact that he had apparently been awake for a couple of hours already. He led Elle out to the dining room and presented her with an exquisite breakfast. Following the morning meal, Hayden beckoned Elle to shower and get ready for an impromptu trip.

"Where are we going?" Elle prodded for clues as she stepped into the shower.

"You will see soon enough," Hayden resisted.

Fifteen minutes later, Elle walked out of the bathroom to find that Hayden had placed an entire outfit on the bed for her. With her curiosity piqued, she slipped on the white dress and then finished getting ready.

Elle walked out the apartment's front door to find Hayden standing in the yard. He was dressed up in accordance with the outfit he had picked for her. Elle could smell his cologne subtly drifting about on the morning breeze.

"What is this?" Elle asked, once again hoping for a morsel of information about their apparent plans.

"Just a couple more minutes," Hayden insisted.

Elle walked over and stood next to Hayden. He waved his hand out in front of them, and a portal opened. Hayden took Elle's hand and led her through.

As she stepped out the other end, Elle looked around to see the ocean in front of her, its waves gently lapping the coast with the telltale sound of the sea caressing her ears. Elle looked around and noticed that the entire beach was empty except for Abby, Dan, and Armond, who stood nearby. Elle looked back at Hayden and finally realized where they were.

"San Diego. The beach we walked along after you took us boating and made us tacos," Elle said, still processing her thoughts. "What are you doing, Hayden?"

"Elle Hensley," Hayden said as he took a knee in the sand. "I've known you for a long time. We grew up as friends, as reading buddies, and as kindred souls in the appreciation for French toast. While I never imagined that our relationship would blossom into this, there is nothing greater in the universe that I could have ever asked for. I am sure that we will last through whatever the future throws at us… because we've been to the future together, and we emerged both unscathed and in love. You fulfill me. You make me a better version of myself."

Elle was visibly surprised. She had no idea that he had been planning this, and their friends had provided no indication that might have given it away. Elle hushed the thoughts running through her head so that he could focus on Hayden's words.

"I cannot wait to begin a family with you. All of these years, perfection was right in front of me. You were right there all along. Elle, there is no higher honor that I could ever achieve than that of you taking my hand."

Elle fidgeted with the anticipation of what she knew was coming next. Abby, Dan, and Armond all moved closer to the couple, their cell phones all out and auspiciously recording. Hayden drew a small box from his pocket and presented the contents to Elle.

"Will you marry me?" he asked her.

"Yes!" Elle screamed as she threw her arms around Hayden.

Hayden placed the ring that he had inconspicuously purchased the day prior during an outing with Dan on Elle's finger. Abby rushed over to add Elle's newly adorned hand to her video footage of the event.

After several minutes of congratulatory remarks and reminiscing about the location, the group headed out for brunch and a day full of activities that Hayden had planned.

ℰℬ ℰℬ ℰℬ ℰℬ ℰℬ ℰℬ

LATER THAT NIGHT:

Elle noticed in the back of her mind the weight of the comforter and the feeling of the soft, yet noticeably crisp, bed sheet against her skin as she lay on top of Hayden. Their bed had never before felt so inviting, so much like home. The connection shared within their kiss made Elle feel whole again. She let the remaining trauma that had haunted her mind up until this point slip away with each passing moment. Elle lost herself in thought, pondering her newly pending nuptials and the life that she and Hayden had created together inside of her.

"I can't wait to meet our child," Elle whispered to Hayden as she gently grazed her hand across his face.

୯୬ ୯୬ ୯୬ ୯୬ ୯୬ ୯୬

ONE WEEK EARLIER:

The hissing sound of escaping air filled the room. A shockwave rattled the structure, knocking fixtures from the walls and loose articles from nearby tables. In the corner, a glass partition retracted, and moments later, Amaris sat up.

After taking a moment to examine his body for the

first time, he collected garments from a nearby drawer and dressed himself. Outside the window, the vast darkness of space beckoned.

Amaris disappeared into a flash of orange and materialized on the surface of a planet. Moving the collection of stones that lay in front of him, he ventured into the small cave to see Kali. Her body was still and surrounded by a translucent protective field.

"Amira. Mother," he spoke to Kali's unconscious body. "I will bring you back. I will avenge you."

Epilogue

Save the Date

Elle casually flipped through the pages of a magazine as she waited for Hayden to park the car and join her and Abby inside the bridal boutique store. The trio were spending an entire day visiting stores, venues, and vendors to create the foundation for Elle and Hayden's wedding plan.

Elle and Abby frolicked through the aisles of dresses and decorations. Hayden happily followed them through the store and took studious notes on their findings. When he found something that caught his eye, Hayden also readily made suggestions to the girls. More than anything, he was delighted to see Elle so passionately excited.

Midday, they arrived at an appointment to view a potential venue in Dana Point. As they pulled into the driveway of the estate, Hayden could see Elle's eyes light up with fascination. The grounds were filled with lush greenery and marble accent pieces. They walked through the front doors of the palatial mansion. Their focus was immediately drawn to the ornate crystal chandelier hanging above the Mediterranean style marble staircases. Hayden looked over at Elle and could already tell from her reaction that this was the place she would want to book for their wedding and reception.

The venue guide continued to show them around the estate. She pointed out the various preparation and entertainment rooms, expansive grounds, stunning swimming pool, and the breathtaking views of the ocean.

"So how do we like it?" the guide asked.

Elle and Abby didn't make any attempts to veil their delight for the location.

"I love it," Elle gushed. "It's a definite yes from me."

"It really is the perfect place, isn't it?" Abby added.

"That's wonderful to hear," the guide responded and then turned to Hayden. "What do you think, sir?"

"I think it's an amazing venue," Hayden admitted. "If Elle says that this is the place, then that settles it for me."

"Perfect," the guide continued. "So let's talk about the date. We usually book pretty far out, but when were you thinking about having your wedding?"

"Well, I was thinking about sometime in April, May, or June of next year," Elle said nervously, knowing that wasn't a substantial amount of lead time.

"Okay, let me take a look at the schedule," the guide said attempting to use a reassuring tone. "It looks like we had a cancellation and there is an opening on the eleventh of May."

"I'm good with that date," Elle replied.

"Alright, I can lock it in for you," the guide continued. "We will just need to get the initial deposit from you to set it in stone."

"Can we?" Elle asked as she looked over at Hayden.

He looked at Elle and could clearly see the bombardment of hopeful gestures intended to beckon him into agreement. Elle was biting her lower lip, had her hands clasped over her chest, and her blue eyes effused a feigned desperation.

"Of course we can," Hayden said while smirking at her methodical ambush of body language. He withdrew his debit card from his wallet and handed it over to the venue guide.

"Thank you!" Elle said with a giddy excitement in her voice.

Elle and Abby ran off to explore the various options

amongst the grounds to stage the ceremony and reception while Hayden took care of the necessary payments and paperwork.

ဢ ဢ ဢ ဢ ဢ ဢ

August 18, 2023

Hayden navigated his car through the streets of Fullerton, while Elle gazed out the window at pedestrians walking along the tree-lined sidewalks.

"Do you ever wonder where people are going when you see them walking around?" Elle inquired.

"Yeah, especially when I'm just sitting around in like a park or something, doing some people watching," Hayden replied. "It's crazy to think that every single person has their own story going on."

"Right?" Elle said in agreement. "All those stories that intertwine with other people's stories."

Hayden made a right turn into the parking lot of an obstetrician's office that had come highly recommended.

"It seems like it was just the other day that I made this appointment," Elle said. "I can't believe it's already time for my first prenatal visit."

"I feel like after spending all that time getting back to the present, everything seems like it happens more quickly now," Hayden agreed.

"Are you ready?" Elle asked.

"I am one hundred percent ready," Hayden said as they exited the car.

"You know, I never thought I would be planning for a wedding and a baby at the same time, but here we are booking venues and visiting doctors," Elle said jokingly as they walked toward the building.

"I hear you," Hayden replied. "But now that we're here, I wouldn't change it for the world."

Hayden grabbed the office door and held it open for Elle. As they walked into the reception area, a staff member greeted them and provided them with the usual first visit forms. After a short wait, the doctor greeted them and led them back to an exam room. Once the initial formalities were completed, the doctor continued to make conversation.

"So, a couple of my colleagues that teach at UCI told me that you are beginning your first year of med school there next month," the doctor said to Hayden.

"Yes, it's coming up quick," Hayden replied. "Elle will also be starting there next month for her Bachelor's degree."

"Oh, that's great. You both get to attend the same

school together," the doctor said. "What are you majoring in, Elle?"

"I'm going to be majoring in physics," Elle replied.

"Good choice. Of course, I'm partial to the sciences," the doctor responded and laughed.

"It's kind of a recent interest that I acquired," Elle admitted.

"Well, I'm sure you'll do great," the doctor assured her. "So, Hayden, have you decided on a specialty yet?"

"I'm not a hundred percent set on anything yet," Hayden said.

"We can always use more good doctors in this field, so keep us in mind. Alright, Elle, everything looks good. We will run the lab tests and then call you with the results. I went ahead and scheduled out your next several visits. The receptionist will have a list for you with all of the dates."

"Okay, thank you so much," Elle replied as she got ready to leave.

"This is my cell phone number," the doctor said while handing Hayden a card. "If either of you has any questions, call me anytime."

"That went really well," Elle said as she and Hayden approached their car.

"Sure did," Hayden agreed and then proceeded to joke

with her. "Just think, in about thirty-two weeks we'll only be getting about two hours of sleep a night."

"Don't remind me!" Elle replied.

ღ ღ ღ ღ ღ ღ

Elle walked into the apartment with a stack of mail and a torn look on her face. She tossed several junk items in the trash before walking up to Hayden with one large envelope prominently held in her hand.

"Lawyer?" Hayden asked after seeing Elle's expression.

"Yep," she confirmed. "Let's see what's in here."

Elle opened the envelope and rifled through dozens of pages, studying some more closely than others. Hayden watched her body language for signs that might allude to the contents.

"You know, it's a good thing you have some of those powers," Elle finally said. "The attorney finally sent over all of the payments for my parent's insurance policies and the deeds to their properties."

"Hey, I just made a couple of corrections and convinced a few people to do the right thing," Hayden replied.

"Yes, you can be very convincing," Elle joked.

After being faced with countless difficulties when they arrived back in the present time, Hayden decided to use several of his powers to correct Elle's birth certificate and information in several government databases. He also pushed thoughts to several key individuals to facilitate Elle receiving everything from her parent's estate.

Although Hayden usually avoided using the powers of Ane'illuminus to accomplish personal endeavors, he made a series of exceptions for what he deemed just purposes. Elle had decided that she wanted to attend college in the fall. However, the unordinary circumstances of their journey back from the year 2027 presented her with trouble. She had been left with no diploma and the application deadlines had passed several months prior.

Hayden easily handled the technicalities with the college admissions department using his powers. Each night thereafter, he helped Elle study to take her GED test. She had expressed her desire to pass the exam as a demonstration of worthiness to herself. Hayden assured her that he knew she was ready, but Elle insisted.

"So, the attorney set up a meeting with the general contractor for next week," Elle said. "They are going to start rebuilding the house in Camarillo at the end of the month.

You and I can go over the plans."

"Sounds good," Hayden replied while checking his phone. "Dan just texted. He and Abby are on their way over."

"Oh, I'll go grab the lists and everything," Elle responded, her tone now more lively.

Once their friends arrived, Elle spread countless samples and cutouts for wedding ideas out on the coffee table. In her hand was a spiral notebook that served as a master plan for the event.

"Okay, first take a look at these," Elle told the group while holding up some cards, with 5/11/24 prominently printed near the top. "The save the date postcards came in yesterday."

"I love them," Abby immediately confessed upon taking hold of one. "They came out just like you wanted."

"I can drop them off at the post office on my way to take Abby back home if you want," Dan offered.

"Thank you," Elle replied. "That would be really helpful."

For the next several hours, the group concentrated on finalizing choices for cakes, clothing, colors, flowers, and songs.

"This planning is a lot easier than I thought it would be," Elle admitted as they wrapped up the day.

"Well, girl you are lucky," Abby said. "If you weren't engaged to Hayden, you'd probably be doing this all yourself. My mother always used to tell me that guys hated wedding planning."

"Hey, what about me?" Dan interjected. "I'm here helping too."

"Yes, I am very proud of you Dan," Abby joked. "Even though I think you still kind of owe it to Elle after that one joke you made back at the restaurant."

"I'm pretty sure I'll be paying off that debt forever," Dan joked back.

಄ ಄ ಄ ಄ ಄ ಄

September 24:

"Happy birthday!" Elle exclaimed as she leapt on top of Hayden and woke him.

"What smells so good?" Hayden asked as he rubbed his eyes and adjusted to the sudden interruption of his slumber.

"Are you talking about me?" Elle joked. "Or are you talking about the breakfast I made for you?"

"Both, naturally," Hayden joked back.

"Are you excited for today?" Elle asked.

"Most definitely," Hayden replied.

After getting ready, Elle and Hayden met up with Abby, Dan, and Armond for lunch.

"Are we all ready for classes to begin at our new school this week?" Abby asked the group, ignoring the fact that Armond had graduated from university long ago.

"I don't know about ready," Elle replied. "But I'm definitely nervous, if that counts."

"You'll do amazing," Abby reassured her. "You should have seen me during my first week at Cal State. I was a walking mess. When I met Dan and Hayden, I'm sure I looked like a lost toddler."

"You did," Dan quickly took the opportunity to joke.

Abby shot him a fake smile and stuck out her tongue. Dan laughed to signify his humorous victory.

"My point, before being rudely interrupted," Abby continued. "Is that you have all of us here to support you. You'll be perfectly fine."

"I'm so thankful for that too," Elle said. "Having all of you at the same school is going to make things so much easier."

"Spring quarter is going to be all kinds of fun," Hayden jumped into the conversation. "We're going to have classes, a baby, and a wedding."

"I don't know how you're doing it all," Dan said with a grin.

"Oh, I'll tell you how," Hayden replied and laughed at Dan's thinly-veiled insinuation. "You and Abby are going to be on speed dial to help us."

"Of course we are," Abby agreed while shoving her elbow into Dan's side. "I can't wait to become Aunt Abby."

As the afternoon turned to evening, the group relocated to a downtown bar that was hosting an open-mic night. As they approached the entrance, Elle began to show her nervousness about gaining entry.

"Just act like you're supposed to be here," Dan told her. "Half the time they don't even card people anyway. That's how Abby manages to get in."

The front door bouncer looked over the group as they walked up. He began to wave them in upon recognizing Hayden and Dan, but then he immediately fixated his gaze on Elle.

"I need your ID," he said as he pointed at Elle.

"Dude, she's obviously not going to be drinking," Dan interjected while pointing at Elle's stomach.

"Still need it," the bouncer replied with an unwavering monotone voice. "She looks like she's twelve and

I'm not getting fired for that."

"She's good to go," Hayden said aloud as he pushed the thought into the bouncer's mind.

"You all enjoy yourselves," he said in a noticeably friendlier tone, as he opened the door and motioned for them to go inside.

"Dude, it's such a good thing that I don't have that power," Dan said as they walked inside.

"Yeah, believe me, we know," Abby said as she pushed him.

A couple hours into the night, the open-mic event began. The group watched several patrons jump on stage and sing various songs, perform short comedy bits, and recite poetry. To their surprise, the announcer called Hayden's name out. As Elle, Dan, and Abby exchanged confused looks, Hayden walked up onto the stage and grabbed an acoustic guitar.

"I've got a couple of songs I wanted to do tonight," Hayden said into the microphone. "This first one is called 'Real Love Can't Pretend.'"

Elle, Abby, and Dan all stood from their seats, gratuitously applauding and hollering as Hayden began strumming the song's intro.

Appendix I

The Ancient Powers

The several powers, or magical abilities, are first seen in use in 54,000 BC (see Agents of Fate: Chapter Three). At that point in time, they became dormant in humans due to a spell performed by Abbas. Their traces were passed on, although they were undetectable to their bearers and the powers unusable.

In 2022, a prophecy came true when Hayden de Vere turned out to be the foretold cognizant one. The appearance of the cognizant one was prophesied by Abbas in a vision approximately two years after the Alva'ci came to Earth. As the bearers of the dormant powers began to die off in 2022, the powers began to manifest once again in their real forms.

Little information is known about the origination of the magical abilities and how or when humans acquired them. It is rumored that there is a book of lore, written by Abbas when he was close to his death, that conveys the secrets that humans used to acquire their magical abilities. Whether or not this book exists is known only to the descendants of Abbas.

The Powers and Their Symbols:

Elemental Powers:

Water ماء   Fire نار

Earth أرض   Air جو

Sub-Elemental Powers:

Light ضوء   Energy طاقة

Shadow ظل   Electricity برق

Non-Elemental Powers:

Ane'illuminus / Thought خاطِر

The Seven Spells نوبات

The Seven Spells:

Abarus - Otherworldly Warriors

Tithethus - The Bindings

Emiratus - Power Amplification

Prophesch'naya Con'di Ashante - Shroud of Darkness

Chantiatus - Protective Forcefields

Youlvasius - Lucky Strikes

Amal Esta Preavius - Energy Portals

The Eighth Spell:

Nelitus Absoritum Malitus - Alva'ci Banishment

The Forbidden Spell:

E'it ad'a Layadänte

The forbidden spell was created by an unknown magic wielder before the time of Abbas. The intended effect of the spell was to bind the fates of two people together. The actual effects turned out to be much more complicated than that. In what was later regarded an act of arrogance and stupidity, the creator of the spell attempted to use it on himself and his wife. They both died immediately. In the years to follow, several other people who regarded themselves as above average in the use of magic also attempted the spell. The result was the same: instantaneous death of all involved. Afterward, the spell was deemed forbidden due to its inherent danger. An attempt was made to purge all records of the words used to cast the spell.

Appendix II

The Prophecies

Abbas recorded several prophecies and visions shortly before he passed away. The following selections are relevant to this entry in The Agents of Fate Series.

The Abassilon Prophecy

53993 BC

At once, you awake and find yourself in a new world,

a new beginning.

The scars of time, though stinging at times,

are dulled from passing years.

Memories of nights that shall never be forgotten

flash through your mind from time to time,

to remind you of all that was had, of all that was lost.

You walk upon the sands,
on the beach of this new land..
journeying to something yet unknown.
You see a girl, standing alone by the water's edge.
Her golden hair flowing in the breeze, her voice fair and sweet.
Her eyes, while calm and inviting,
also piercing and hiding much behind them.

As you walk nearer, flashes of destiny
race through your mind like precognitive deja vu.
What path is coming to emerge?
You can feel it in your bones,
if you approach her, a piece of your life will be hers.

They've called you many things...
they focused on the darkness that swirled around you.
And though they were mistaken,
as magnificence can oft be mistook for darkness,
they never understood.
But as you look onward toward the girl,
you can see the light from within her.

...and the light shall mingle with the darkness, and together
they shall shine with a brilliance both dazzling and fearsome.

———

She turns to see you and you look into her eyes.
Suddenly you understand,
and together you walk toward the city.

~~E'it ad'a layadänte~~
We shall share this path

The Prophecy of Hindrant Salvas
53980 BC

Pacing the grounds, hollow footsteps echo into oblivion.
Turning round, facing the reality of duplicity.

Into the waters, knee-deep. The rip current drawing you in.
The seduction that you both play on each other
is providential.

What can you have?
Is it greater than anything you've been given?
What remains to be seen,
shall determine the course of revisionist history.

Turning a corner into the halls of life yet written.
Through the doorway and into an empty room.

We have come to dance here,
a dance careful and indifferent.
Setting the night ablaze with aberrant passions.
The world outside these windows, vast and insignificant.
Who you are at dusk is not the you of dawn.

Reaching a precipice, fraught with lasting decisions.
How do you get what you want,
when what you want is everything?

Appendix III

The Books of Lore

Abbas wrote several books that were passed down to the firstborn of each generation of his family. These books contained the lore concerning the Agents of Fate. The current keeper of the books of lore is Armond el-Hashem. Among the known volumes are:

The Conqueror الفاتح

An account of the arrival of the Alva'ci on Earth. This book contains first-hand accounts from Abbas, Ahjiamed, Koshili, and dozens of other members of their village. Also included are charts and drawings depicting the creature, a sky chart detailing where the Alva'ci entered the atmosphere, and a description of the orange rock that the creature's armor consisted of.

Prophecies and Visions نبوءات ورؤى

After the victory obtained over the Alva'ci in 54,000 BC, Abbas began to have visions pertaining to the nature of the Agents of Fate and future events that concerned those that held the remnants of power. This book of lore is a collection of the visions and prophecies that Abbas made until his death at the age of 387. One of the most prominent prophecies included was The Parisifian Prophecy. This prophecy foretold the eventual appearance of the Cognizant One, an Agent of Fate that was unique in their abilities and would come at a time in history when the Alva'ci may possess the ability to rise again.

Powers and Practices القدرات والمهارات
(aka Abilities and Skills)

Written very late in the life of Abbas, this book of lore's existence is only rumored. It is said that this book includes detailed explanations of how humans first acquired magical abilities. Details of each magical power and its uses are included, ranging from the simplest forms to advanced techniques that came with aptitude and skill. The book includes a detailed account of the power of Ane'illuminus and the achievements made by those that mastered the power within their lifetimes. A section of the lore includes an account of how Abbas and a handful of others were able to artificially extend their lives to seemingly unnatural ages through the masterful use of the magical powers. Finally, Abbas included warnings concerning the use of The Forbidden Spell (which is mentioned in The Abassilon Prophecy, but with the words crossed out to prevent its use). The warnings also included several accounts of various magic users that attempted the spell only to meet their immediate deaths.

About the Author

Tony Contratto writes books, this much we know. In his free time, he is also a small business owner and nonprofit director. Tony's philosophy is that the most gripping and immersive tales happen in our imagination. In the spirit of that ideology, Tony spent several years formulating the story of his first novel within his head, before ever putting the proverbial pen to paper. Originally from Southern California, Tony now resides in Lake Havasu City, Arizona. Visit Tony at his website and follow him on social media at contrattos.net

Coming Soon

Elle yelled across the expanse of the apartment with a decidedly surprised pitch. "Hayden, come here quick!"

As sudden as her seemingly random yet emergent beckoning, Hayden appeared in the dining room where Elle was eating her breakfast. His face changed from potential worry to inquisitive wonder when he saw that Elle's expression was one of frantic joy.

Join Hayden, Elle, Abby, and Dan as
The Agents of Fate Series
continues with the **third** installment:

The Quickening

"Some call it Powers and Practices.
We call it The Book of Damnation."

ༀ ༀ ༀ ༀ ༀ ༀ

Sign up for the Insider Email Newsletter and receive
a FREE exclusive copy of the prequel story
AOF: The Distant Shadow
at
agentsoffate.com

More To Read